PROJECT ARK

ARK

LT Gibbs

PROJECT ARK

First published in 2014 by LT Gibbons
LTGibbons@outlook.com

ISBN: 978-0-646-92580-6

Cover by Nodding Dog

www.LTGibbonsAuthor.com

This book is dedicated to my Mum and Dad.

For bringing me into this world.
For making me the person that I am today.
And for being infallible in their support
for every crazy idea I've ever had.
Especially this one.

Chapter 1

I knew instantly that something was wrong. It was the expression on my mother's face that gave it away.

A half unwrapped gift lay frozen in my hands as I looked up at the slender figure in the doorway. She smiled down at me, curled up next to the glowing and crackling fire. Guilt seeped through her sad eyes.

"That was The Journal on the phone," she said, as if I hadn't guessed.

I remained silent. I already knew what she was going to say.

She paused. "They need me to follow a story... It's quite big." Her eyes lit up then.

"On Christmas day?" I spat. All resolve to remain calm evaporating.

She reeled back, just a fraction, but it was noticeable. I watched her rearrange her features and adjust her posture. Almost as if she were reminding herself that she was the one in charge here. Not her fourteen year old daughter.

"Mia, you know I can't afford to turn down work. Not since your father left us."

She'd used that line so many times that I think she almost believed it herself. I used to believe it too. Now I know it's purely that she loves her job. The thrill of the story. Unmasking the truth. Helping to bring about justice. I didn't argue with her; it wasn't worth the trouble. Her mind was already made up.

"Has Dad called this morning?" I asked, placing the unopened gift on the floor. I wasn't feeling particularly festive any more.

"Early this morning. I didn't want to wake you," she said, looking at me apprehensively. "He was just about to leave on a seven day trek. He won't be contactable for a while. He... he sends his love."

My throat tightened. This wasn't anything new or out of the ordinary. My parents divorced when I was around six years old, and it was rare that Dad and I got to see each other. He'd retired early and always seemed to be travelling somewhere in the world, trekking through a rain forest or climbing a mountain. But it didn't hurt any less.

I focused my eyes on the Christmas tree to avoid my mother's gaze. Presents that looked like they'd been wrapped by an animal were piled up beneath the garishly decorated tree. Aesthetics was not one of my mother's strong points. It wasn't exactly that she didn't care. She just believed there were more important things in life to worry about.

"I've spoken to Ellie's mum already. They'd love to have you spend the day with them."

My mood shifted at the thought of my best friend.

"If you hurry, I can drop you off on my way to work."

The icy wind hit me as I stepped out into the cold and I shivered. I could see my own breath in the air and made rings with my mouth to distract myself from the plummeting temperature. The aging trees lining the driveway were bare. Icicles hung from their branches, like a jewelled necklace dripping through slender fingers. Frost dusted the grass, casting a diamond-white sheen across the garden. I rushed towards to the waiting car, the low winter sun glinting off the silver bonnet.

My mum sounded the horn and waved goodbye from the car as I walked through the gate. Ellie flung open the door almost instantly and barrelled me into a hug that left me choking for breath.

"Merry Christmas, my surrogate sister," she said, holding me tightly and rocking me in her arms.

Mrs Fielding called out from the hallway, "Girls, you're letting all the heat escape. Come inside and shut the door, quickly." She ushered us in and put her arm around me. "Merry Christmas, dear. We'll look after you, don't you worry," she said smiling at me sympathetically.

"You always do." I smiled back bleakly.

"Miranda is a dear old friend of mine. I'd do anything for you and your mum. You know that…" She squeezed my shoulder. "Now, are you ready to spread some festive cheer amongst the homeless?" she asked, noticeably changing the subject.

"Of course. I'm looking forward to it," I said. Sometimes all you needed was a little perspective in life. I really didn't have anything to complain about.

Ellie linked her arm through mine and squeezed. "Jack Faraday will be there today…"

My heart lifted a little, just hearing his name.

"He likes you, you know," she said, nudging me in the ribs.

I blushed. "He's like that with everyone."

"It's different with you though, I can tell."

I smiled. Ellie always knew the right thing to say.

I barely had time to think for the next few hours. Crowds of people were already queuing up outside the homeless shelter when we arrived, and we didn't stop until everyone had been fed. I'd been partnered with Jack, and although there was little opportunity for conversation, I'd felt a surge of electricity every time our eyes met or we bumped hands. At the end of the day, I felt overwhelmed with an array of emotion. I was exhausted, but happy, and ultimately grateful for everything I had.

Ellie's parents dropped me home just as the sun was starting to set. Smoke drifted from the brick chimney, promising warmth inside, and I hurried towards the house.

I let myself in and began unravelling my scarf, letting it fall to the floor as I made my way through the hallway. Soft murmurs drifted from the living room, indicating that my mum was home. I hooked my bag onto the banister and kicked off my boots one by one, leaving a trail of apparel in my wake.

I quietly pushed open the door to the living room and peered through the gap. My mum was sat on the suede sofa, her legs tucked beneath her. Her blonde hair, streaked with soft grey, was clipped back into a neat ponytail. A glass of red wine sat untouched on the coffee table in front of her. A documentary blared from the television set, and her eyes were trained in its direction, but it was apparent her mind was elsewhere.

She looked up as I slid in next to her on the sofa, and her brow furrowed. My mother and I had been cursed with the same misfortune. Our faces had always been like open books. All of our thoughts and emotions were perfectly visible, without either of us ever having to utter a word.

"What's wrong?" I asked, the pit of my stomach stirring with worry.

"Mia… I don't even know how to say this. Where to start…"

"Is everyone ok? Grandma..?"

She put her hand over mine, perhaps to reassure herself more than anything. "Everybody's fine, nobody's sick."

"Then what is is?" I asked, searching her eyes for the answers.

"I have to go away… for a while."

"How long's a while?" I asked suspiciously.

"I'm not sure right now. It could be months. Maybe even longer."

"Well, I'll come with you then."

"No, darling, it's not safe."

"Why? Where are you going?"

She took a deep breath. "To the Middle East. I've been offered a promotion…"

"This is to do with work? Again?" I interrupted, blood rushing to my face in anger.

"They've asked me to be the acting war correspondent. I couldn't turn it down."

"Because we need the money so desperately?"

She looked at me pleadingly but didn't answer my question.

"When do you have to leave?" I asked, still uncomprehending.

"In the next few days. As soon as I find somewhere for you to stay."

"Why can't I stay here?"

"Darling, you're fourteen years old, I can't leave you home alone."

"Well, I'll stay with Dad, then."

"I can't get hold of your father, sweetheart. I wouldn't even know where to start trying to find him."

"Can't I stay with Ellie?" My desperation must have been audible by that point.

"I couldn't ask that of Ellie's mum. Not for that length of time."

"I can't believe you're doing this to me." I narrowed my eyes at her, full of hurt. "Merry Christmas, Mum."

She looked at me as if I'd stabbed her in the heart. I backed out of the room and pulled the door tightly shut behind me. I picked up my boots and scarf and crept up to my bedroom. I crawled into bed and tears began to roll down my cheeks at the unfairness of it all. I lay there with the covers over my head, sobbing quietly to myself.

After a while, a soft rapping at the door awoke me from my maudlin reverie.

"Mia?" The sound of my mother's voice made my stomach tighten instantly. I pulled the covers more firmly around my head and silently willed her to go away. "Mia, I know you're awake," she said, opening the door slowly.

"Mum, I can't talk to you right now. Just… leave me alone." The words broke as a sob escaped my mouth.

She pulled the covers from my face and sat down on the edge of the bed, looking at me sadly. I pulled myself up and brushed my tangled hair out of my eyes. I prepared myself for the worst.

"I've spoken to your great grandfather and, I've

decided… I think it's best that you go and stay with him for a while," she said with a heavy sigh.

"In New Mexico?" My eyes narrowed.

"Yes. I think it will be good for you. I would have loved the opportunity to see some of the world at your age."

"How long will I be staying with him for?"

"You know your great grandfather has been asking for you since you turned fourteen. Almost a year now. I didn't think it was the right thing to do, not until you'd finished school at least. Or university even. But I really don't have any other option."

"You're not answering my question," I said, frowning, and sitting up very straight. There was something about my mother's expression. It was almost as if she were grieving, and that made me concerned. "How long will I be staying with my great grandfather for?"

She paused and then looked away. "Indefinitely, Mia. You'll be going to live with your great grandfather indefinitely."

"Are you serious?!" I burst out. "You're taking me out of school? Mum, *all* of my friends are here. My whole world! You can't do this to me…" I pleaded and starting crying uncontrollably while Mum just stroked my hair softly and let me sob.

"We'll talk more about this when you've calmed down," she said, once the hysterics had softened to sniffs and gulps of air. She lay me down, pulled the blankets up around my heaving shoulders and kissed me on the forehead. I fought every urge in my body to pack my bags and run away, but all the emotion had wiped me out and I fell quickly into a deep, dreamless sleep.

Once the decision had been made, everything seemed to fall into place almost instantly. There wasn't enough time for me to wallow in my own misery so I'd had to snap out of it pretty quickly. Mum decided she was going to rent the house out while we were away, so we had to pack up all of our belongings and move them into storage. I spent hours seeing school friends and enduring teary goodbyes. The worst was leaving Ellie and Jack. I didn't get the chance to see my dad before I left. Although I felt there was probably more likelihood I'd bump into him in New Mexico than at home.

It was still dark when I awoke on my last morning. I hauled myself out of bed and shuffled sleepily towards the window, peering out from behind a chink in the curtains. The forecast was for snow and I silently pleaded with the gods, and every other higher power, to let us be snowed in. Or at least have the flight cancelled due to bad weather. But there wasn't a snowflake in sight. In fact, the sky was completely clear and the trees were still. It looked like it was going to be a sunny, calm day, in stark contrast to my mood.

The journey to the airport felt unusually long. I stared resolutely out of the window and tried to avoid any conversation with my mum, but she pushed ahead regardless.

"I'm sure you must hate me right now, Mia, but I

promise, in the long run, this will be for the best."

I remained tight lipped, my eyes following the barren trees as they flew past the window.

Mum sighed in mild exasperation. "I know you think the world of your father, Mia, and I wouldn't change that... But he's had a pretty good deal. He got to have the beautiful daughter, who is there at his beck and call, who hangs on his every word... And then at the same time, he's been able to carry on with his life as if he were a bachelor, with not a single responsibility. I've given you everything, Mia. I've sacrificed so much for you. And now it's my turn. I need to live my life too."

It felt as though my mother was largely trying to justify her actions to herself, so I didn't feel the need to say anything. She eventually fell silent and we didn't speak for the remainder of the journey.

Mum was teary at the airport but tried not to show it by taking over everything. She unpacked and repacked my case repeatedly so that we didn't have to pay for excess baggage. I eventually had to relent and leave two of my heaviest books behind. Mum left me at the departure lounge and, refusing to make eye contact, hugged me tightly until I started to gasp for air. I was still too angry at her to feel truly sad, but a lump formed in my throat and I squeezed her back briefly, before fleeing towards security.

I'd resolved to be stoic about the situation. After all, I couldn't do anything about it; I might as well try and deal with it sooner rather than later. I pushed all thoughts of my friends, family and home out of my mind and tried to focus on what lay ahead. As I boarded the plane, my stomach somersaulted into my chest and I had to swallow repeatedly to stop myself from vomiting. I hurried to my seat and immersed myself in the inflight magazine in a bid to suppress my racing mind.

I alternated between dozing and watching movies during the flight - anything to keep my waking mind occupied. I was almost going stir-crazy by the time we began our descent into Albuquerque. I gazed out of the window as we flew down over the jagged Rocky Mountains, past vast sprawling suburbia, and then sweeping planes of desert, before hitting the runway without a jolt. I was one of the last to disembark from the plane and reluctantly joined the other passengers as they filed across the tarmac, towards the low level concrete monolith of a terminal building.

We were greeted on entry by a sea of nondescript faces carrying name boards. I skim-read the signs - an assortment of colourful 'welcome home' posters, then others more formal and business-like. I caught my breath. There, typed out impersonally onto plain white cardboard, was my own name: Mia McAdams. I looked up to see the sign was held by an unsmiling tall man, sporting a crew cut, sunglasses and a very well-pressed military uniform.

"This way, Miss McAdams," my escort spoke quickly and almost robotically. He held out his hand and gestured to a golf buggy behind him. I slid into the white vehicle unquestioningly, dazed from a combination of the journey, jetlag and the unfamiliar surroundings. I knew my great grandfather was fairly important, but this seemed a little overboard. My luggage had already been loaded efficiently onto the back of the buggy and we sped across the terminal, narrowly missing weary travellers carting their luggage behind them. It slowly began to dawn on me that we weren't actually heading towards the exit. An idea that was solidified as we made a sharp left and started to drive straight towards a set of glass doors. The doors snapped open just inches before the buggy reached them and suddenly we were out on the tarmac, speeding directly towards a sleek black private jet.

Chapter 2

"Everything ok, Miss?" My escort's voice, at least two octaves lower than any human voice I'd ever heard before, jolted me out of some kind of shock–induced paralysis. I realised I was practically cowering behind my hands, and lowered them quickly to my sides. I cleared my throat to be sure anything I said was actually audible to the naked ear.

"Where are we going exactly? And where's my great grandfather? I thought he lived in Albuquerque?" The questions tumbled out of my mouth almost as they appeared in my thoughts.

"Not quite, Miss McAdams, not quite." His face was expressionless, his eyes hidden behind mirrored aviator sunglasses.

"That doesn't answer my questions," I said suspiciously.

"It's top secret information, Miss Mia. You'll learn

all you need to know soon enough." He leapt athletically out of the buggy and picked up my luggage, almost in one clear movement. "Follow me."

I had to jog a little to catch up, and followed him up the stairs of the gleaming black gulfstream jet. I stepped inside and was almost struck dumb. I'd barely flown at all in my life, let alone in something like this. The plane was more how I'd imagined a cool private club to look. Black leather seats were grouped casually around mirrored coffee tables, and a curved marble bar occupied the length of the plane, lined with dark leather bar stools. Low mood-lighting added to the effect, while soft elevator-style music played through the Bose sound system.

I wriggled into one of the vast seats and my escort came and sat silently opposite me. I couldn't tell if he was looking at me or not behind the aviators but I stared at him unblinkingly all the same. It didn't seem to ruffle him; his eyes could even have been closed. I'd just turned to look out of the window instead, when he spoke.

"You can call me Lieutenant Marshall, Miss McAdams." He took his glasses off and looked at me meaningfully with deep brown eyes. "Everything is going to be ok. You can trust me."

I narrowed my eyes for a moment, before softening quickly. "Whatever you say, Lieutenant." Before I had chance to sit back and make the most of the luxury, the crew was being asked to prepare for landing, almost immediately after take off. I peered out of the window as we began our descent; the jet trained towards a gap in between two jagged mountains. It was like something out of an old Russian spy movie.

We flew low over ripples of white sand and then landed quickly and smoothly, in front of an ugly collection of ramshackle, beige stone buildings.

"We haven't got long, Miss McAdams," started the lieutenant as we moved towards the exit. "You'll need to move fast and follow instructions."

I nodded and followed quickly behind. Two women in white coats were waiting at the bottom of the plane to greet us and they ushered me quickly into a clinical-looking building. I was led to an office and asked to sit down. The lieutenant saluted me and then closed the door quietly behind himself.

I was left alone with a burly-looking woman with thick, wide-set eyebrows and a dimple in each cheek. We looked at each other for a while and it felt like I was being examined, but for what, I had no idea. Long after the silence had become uncomfortable, the woman spoke.

"My name is Doctor Mary Matheson," she began hesitantly. " I'm the psychologist here at Holloman."

"I don't understand," I said, getting out of my chair. "Am I being sectioned? No wait, worse, have I been sent to military school?!" I was suddenly fearful that I hadn't been sent to see my great grandfather at all. That my mother had actually lost it and decided I needed a military education. Doctor Matheson stood up carefully and reached out, gently patting my shoulder.

"No, no, Mia," she said soothingly. "Sit back down please." She stood with a firm but gentle hand on each of my shoulders. "This is a top secret military operation. Before you are sent to your great grandfather, you need to undergo tests and training. Normally it would take several weeks, but if we can fast track you, we will. That's the purpose of this psychological assessment."

I sat back down. I couldn't even begin to put the jigsaw pieces together. I was at an absolute loss. I had no idea where my great grandfather was, or what any of this was about. Suddenly I felt very alone, tired and more than a little bewildered. Tears started to form in the corners of my eyes and Doctor Matheson quickly moved over to put an arm around my shoulders.

"I know this must be very confronting for you, and believe me, it will all start to make sense very soon. What you're about to learn is going to affect your entire grip on reality and we need to make sure you're emotionally and physically equipped to deal with it. It must seem unorthodox, but this operation is so sensitive that we can't take any risks."

I took a deep breath and sat upright in my chair, gathering all the emotional strength I could muster. "Ok… What do you need me to do?"

The rest of the day went by in a whirl. I filled out countless forms, completed an assortment of personality tests, drew pictures and answered questions about peculiar images being held up in front of me. After the psychological assessment, I was ushered into the care of the second doctor who'd greeted us off the plane.

Doctor Edith Daniels was more stern-looking and very wrinkled, with grey hair that had been pulled tightly into a bun. She efficiently led me through the physical examination as if I were a piece of meat on a production line. My height and weight were measured, then my eye sight, hearing and reactions were all checked. I almost kicked her in the head when she hit my knee with the wooden hammer. I was swept through a CT scan and then spun around in a space-age vertical x-ray tube. I gave what looked like litres of blood, followed by urine samples. I was at the point where I couldn't take any more prodding and poking, when Doctor Daniels enveloped me in a thick, white robe and led me to my room. She held the door open to a very small white cube. A metal bed was tightly made up with white sheets that had hospital corners. A small table was positioned in the corner of the room, already set with a glass of water, a plate overflowing with fresh fish and lush, brightly-coloured vegetables, and a small bowl of fruit and yoghurt.

"Eat up and sleep well; you'll need all your strength for tomorrow, Miss Mia," Doctor Daniels said, a little sternly, and then closed the door behind her. I hadn't realised with all the day's activity that I was ravenous. I devoured the food that had been left out for me and then flopped onto the bed. I was so tired that I was almost beyond curious about what tomorrow would unfold. I wriggled into the sheets, flicked off the light and instantly fell into the deepest sleep of my life. A fact that I would be undeniably thankful for the next day, for what I was about to learn was going to turn my world completely upside down.

The next day began normally. Well, as normally as could be when a girl finds herself unexpectedly captive at a military base camp. The dark room was windowless, so when a bell sounded that it was time to get up, I awoke in panic, having no clue where I was or what time it was. My automatic waking reaction was to walk over to the window to check the weather outside, but the four blank walls stared back at me unmovingly.

The lights flicked on and a moment later, a clipped voice drifted from a hidden speaker system, making me start. "Good morning, Miss McAdams. Please report to Doctor Daniels in room 5102 at 07:00 hours sharp."

I rummaged through my backpack for my phone and saw that it was ten minutes to seven. I quickly brushed my teeth and pulled on the training clothes that had been left out for me. Wearing my military regulation shorts, trainers and a white t-shirt, I made my way down the corridor to room 5102.

Doctor Daniels looked me up and down as I stood apprehensively in the doorway. "Good morning, Mia. How are you feeling today?"

"Much better, thank you," I said, not moving away from the door.

The doctor studied me for a few moments before speaking again, "We have a few more tests to run this morning and then we'll go over your results after lunch. If everything is in order, we'll put plans in place for your departure and you'll be out of here by morning." The doctor gestured for me to join her at her desk and I moved cautiously towards her. "The purpose of this morning is to test your fitness and agility. We'll start with checking your body fat; hold out your left arm out for me."

The doctor picked up a pair of giant plastic tweezers and then proceeded to squeeze the skin on my triceps and biceps. She then took readings from my waist and shoulder blades, jotting down the measurements. "You have a very low body fat percentage. Are you particularly active?"

"Actually, not at all." I blushed. "My mum says it's something to do with our fast metabolism," I added a little guiltily.

The doctor shook her head in disapproval. "I'm now going to test how your heart responds to stress. I'm going to take your vitals first and then ask you to step onto the treadmill."

She took my pulse, temperature and blood pressure unsmilingly, noting down figures without speaking. She then stuck electrodes to my chest, shoulders and hips, before directing me to the treadmill. She started it nice and slowly and I thought that wasn't so bad. And then I spent the next ten minutes in some kind of personal torture hell, where the doctor alternated between increasing the incline and the speed every three minutes. My cheeks felt like they were on fire and I was dripping in sweat before the doctor asked me to get off the treadmill. She handed me a glass of water and moved over to her computer to check the results.

"Well, that all seems normal," she said. "You can see the lieutenant now. He's in the gym next door."

I stood there gasping for air, my shoulders heaving. The thought of more fitness tests was alarming, but Doctor Daniels scared me a little, so I put down my glass and left the room quickly and quietly.

Lieutenant Marshall was waiting for me in the gym with a wide smile. "How are you today, Miss McAdams? Feeling refreshed?"

"Much better today, thank you," I said sheepishly. "Although I feel like these tests are a little unnecessary. I can tell you straight off I'm not fit or agile in the slightest... My idea of exercise is climbing the stairs to go to bed."

The lieutenant laughed heartily. "I'm not worried, Mia. It's just protocol... Alright, let's get started!" He blew his whistle and I jumped. The gym suddenly came into focus and my heart sank, right down to my knees. The next half hour was one of the worst in my life. I was first subjected to an agonising 20 metre shuttle run, before starting on the agility test. An obstacle course had been laid out around the gym and Lieutenant Marshall stood at the finish line with a stop clock in one hand and a whistle in the other. The whistle blew and I ran towards the first hurdle. I climbed mesh and wire fences of various heights, crawled through thin tubing, balanced precariously on the gymnastics bar, leapt across a 1.5 metre gap, ran through strategically placed debris, clambered over more hurdles, dragged a punch bag for 20 metres, squeezed myself through a near impossible gap and then sprinted 100 metres to the finish line. I got to the end and bent double, barely able to breathe let alone speak.

"Very good Mia, very good! Now let's do it again." I looked up in horror at the lieutenant's words and he broke into laughter. "Just kidding." I collapsed on the floor with relief, still incapable of speaking. "Now go and get into the shower. I have a meeting with the assessment team next. Hopefully we'll soon be in a position to move you onto stage two later today."

I stepped out of what felt like the most rejuvenating shower I'd ever experienced and circled the white robe around me. There was a sharp rap at the door before a young woman wearing a black and white server's uniform backed into the room carrying a wide steel tray. She unloaded the contents onto the table in the corner and then quietly left the room without making eye contact. I sat down at the table and eyed the feast hungrily. Herbed sausages, avocado, spinach, mushroom, tomato and eggs spilled over the plate. A vague thought flitted across my mind that I was being plumped for slaughter but I quickly let it disappear, digging in as if it were my last meal all the same.

A second after I took my last bite, almost as if I were being watched, a voice came through the speakers. "Miss McAdams, the assessment team will see you now. Please make your way to room 5102."

I quickly changed into a fresh set of clothes, hopping on each leg to slip on the pumps while sliding through the door. I reached the room and knocked, before opening the door and cautiously poking my head through the gap. I could see the team sitting around a table, looking relaxed and at ease. I let out the breath that I hadn't realised I'd been holding and felt the tension leave my shoulders. I was relieved. There was nothing to worry about. All this uncertainty was about to be over, and I'd soon be at home with my great grandfather.

"Come in and join us, Mia," the lieutenant said. "Take a seat." He gestured to the only available chair at the table, and I slid into it, looking at the others expectantly. Doctor Daniels was the first to speak, her sharp staccato tones softer than usual.

"Mia, we're pleased to inform you that you have passed all of your examinations. You have been deemed mentally, emotionally and physically fit, and are able to proceed to the next phase." Doctor Daniels' features creased into a smile, and I found myself joining her.

Doctor Matheson interjected carefully, "Now, Mia, Lieutenant Marshall is going to bring you up to speed with the operation and you will need to pay close attention. I will stay with you throughout, so if you have any questions or concerns, please don't be afraid to speak up."

Doctor Daniels quietly left the room as the lieutenant slid a non disclosure agreement across the table. I eyed it warily.

"We can't take any chances, Mia; this operation is top secret. What you are about to learn... You won't be able to disclose to anyone, not even your family or closest friends. If any of this information is leaked to the public, you will face life imprisonment. Do you understand the severity of the consequences?" I nodded dumbly and felt my stomach perform a backflip. "I need you to read this very carefully and then sign it before we begin."

The lieutenant handed me a pen and I began to painstakingly read the contract. The room was completely silent, bar the sounds of a clock ticking loudly and methodically on the back wall. I paused at the end of the lengthy document, a thousand thoughts flashing through my mind. I was terrible at keeping secrets... But this was serious. I could end up in jail. I gripped the pen tightly, held my breath and signed quickly before I could change my mind. I pushed the document towards Lieutenant Marshall and then sat back in the seat with my arms folded.

The lieutenant cleared his throat loudly and then began. "There is no easy way to tell you this, Mia, so I'll just launch right in." He paused, eyeing me carefully before continuing hesitantly. "Your great grandfather, Herbert McAdams, was a noble man. An explorer, an adventurer, and a pioneer... In the late 1940s, he was selected to be part of a highly classified operation. An operation known as Project Ark." I watched the lieutenant silently, wondering where all this was going. He took a breath.

"After the first nuclear weapons were used in warfare, towards the end of the second world war, the Earth's major leaders held an emergency security conference. It was agreed that something needed to be done in order to safeguard the future of the human race... and so, a core team of the world's elite was immediately assembled and work began colonising a recently discovered planet. A planet we named Usonia."

My jaw practically dropped to the floor. "I'm sorry, I'm not sure I heard you properly. What did you just say?" I stared dumbfounded, my mouth still open. Doctor Matheson shuffled in her seat, watching me closely.

The lieutenant paused, gathering his thoughts and then spoke slowly and carefully, "In the 1940s, governments from all over the world joined forces to select and train a core team of the world's best scientists, engineers, doctors, architects, teachers and athletes. In 1949, the team boarded Starship Beta and was launched into space. Three days later, they landed on Usonia and became the first intelligent species to inhabit the planet. We refer to these individuals as the founding fathers, and Mia, your great grandfather was one of them."

I sat transfixed. "But, but... I thought... Wasn't..? Didn't..?" I trailed off, at a loss for words. I was scanning my brain for everything I'd been taught or read about history and astronomy, but this didn't seem to fit.

Doctor Matheson spoke up with a carefully

measured voice, "Take all the time you need to process this, Mia. We know it contradicts everything you thought was true. You'll have a lot of questions, and we're happy to answer them all for you, in time."

We sat in silence for a while as I tried to digest this new reality. A complete 180 on everything I thought I knew about the universe. "So what you're saying is… there's this planet that exists, called Usonia. And it's habitable. We know this because, my great grandfather was one of the first people to inhabit the planet…" And then it hit me. "Wait. Is that where I'm going? Usonia?" I stared in horror.

"Yes, Mia," Lieutenant Marshall spoke quietly, almost soothingly. "You will be flying out to Usonia to be with your great grandfather. The ship is scheduled for launch in 21 hours."

I stood up abruptly, sending my chair crashing to the ground, my eyes wide with shock and realisation. "You're sending me to *live* on another *planet*?"

Chapter 3

I turned and fled the room, slamming the door behind me. I spun left and then right, searching down vast empty white corridors. Security guards punctuated each end of the hallway, and with the prospect of empty desert on the other side of each door, I had little choice other than to return to my windowless cell. I pushed open the door and then flung myself onto the bed. I grabbed the pillow, pressed it over my mouth and then screamed and screamed, until the sobs began to escape. No-one disturbed me. I was allowed to mourn for my former life for what felt like hours. I lay in bed curled up in a ball and stared blankly at the white wall in front of me.

I'd thought that moving to another country was bad enough, but another planet? I couldn't even tell anyone where I was going. No-one would be able to visit me. Would I even be able to communicate with people on Earth once I was up there? I couldn't imagine living on another planet. The idea of going to a new school in a new country was anxiety-inducing. Starting school on a new planet was off the charts.

I must have drifted into sleep because I was awoken by the sound of soft knocking. Doctor Matheson slowly pushed open the door. "Do you mind if I come in, Mia?" I nodded glumly and sat up in bed. The doctor perched next to me and eyed me sympathetically. "How are you feeling?"

I looked at her without speaking, my eyes wide and teary. I was lost for words, probably for the first time in my life. I was feeling so many things, most of them new or difficult to explain.

"You must be feeling overwhelmed, scared... lost, even. But that's understandable, Mia. It's ok to feel this way, especially under the circumstances. Can I do anything for you? Do you need anything?"

Suddenly I knew exactly what I needed. The words burst from my mouth, "Could I phone my dad?" I waited expectantly.

The doctor paused. "I'm not sure that's a good idea. You won't be able to tell him anything; remember you signed the NDA..." She trailed off and looked at me with a concerned expression. "Look, if you're absolutely confident you can speak to him without letting anything slip..."

"I promise I won't say anything I'm not supposed to. I just need to hear his voice."

She relented. "Alright then, follow me." Doctor

Matheson stood up and led me to her office. She gestured towards the phone and then discretely moved to the opposite side of the room, making a show of filing paperwork.

I hesitantly picked up the phone and dialled the number. He didn't pick up straight away and the dial tone was strange, like he was in a foreign county. Then eventually, there was a click and muffled background noise.

"Dad?"

"Mia, is that you?" came the most familiar voice. One that made everything seem ok. A voice that could fix everything.

"Dad! It's so good to hear your voice."

"Mia… How are you, sweetheart? What are you doing right now?"

"I'm, um, I'm ok… I'm in New Mexico," the words spilled out of my mouth. "I've come to stay with Great Granddad for a little while. Mum's had to go to the Middle East for work and I didn't get a chance to say goodbye to you. I just really felt like I needed to speak to you…"

"New Mexico? Well that sounds like an adventure, you lucky thing. I'm so sorry I missed you, sweetheart. I just got back from trekking the Spanish Pyrenees this afternoon. I wish you were here, kiddo."

"Me too, Dad, me too."

"You're sure everything's ok?"

"Yeah, I'd better go, this is probably costing Herb a fortune. Try not to eat too much paella; you need to keep that middle aged spread of yours in check."

"You're a cheeky little lady… Although you're probably right. Take care, princess, remember I love you."

"I love you too, Dad."

I hung up the phone, feeling terrible for lying to my dad, but glad I'd had the chance to speak to him before I left. I took a deep breath and then looked at Doctor Matheson. "Alright, let's get on with this. What next?"

The doctor smiled and looked a little relieved. "Well, next you'll need to sit a crash course on space travel."

"*Crash* course?" I swallowed hard.

"Maybe I should have gone with 'intensive'." She smiled wryly. "Alright, let's go…"

The rest of the afternoon was vaguely thrilling. I'd pushed the reality of the situation to the back of my mind and instead, focused on preparing myself to travel into space. It was crazy, really. Millions of kids dream of this kind of thing and it was actually happening to me. I practised getting in and out of my space suit, learned about the kind of food I was going to be eating for the next three days and experienced being in zero gravity. That part was really fun. Although the freeze dried baby food wasn't so much. Lastly, we went through basic emergency response training, which was nothing short of terrifying.

"There's really nothing for you to worry about, Mia." The lieutenant reassured me. "We send spaceships up every week to deliver the mail and carry government officials. They visit periodically for security meetings and to check on the planet's progress. It's a fail-safe mode of transport. Now go and get a good night's sleep. You have a big day ahead of you tomorrow."

The next morning passed by in a blur. I was fed a huge nutritious breakfast that I demolished, not having any idea where my next real meal was coming from. I soaked in the bath, submerging my head under the soapy water, and trying not to think past each individual step that was taking me to my new life. Anything beyond that filled me with a mild, rising panic. I towel-dried my hair and stepped into a white Lycra one-piece. I scrutinised my pale, naked face in the mirror. My grey eyes, the colour of the Irish Sea, looked back at me, expressionless. A scattering of light freckles dusted my almost translucent cheeks. There seemed little point in putting on makeup to sit on a space shuttle for the next three days so I twisted my hair into a bun, inhaled deeply and then stepped away from the mirror.

One by one, each of the team stopped by to offer words of wisdom, encouragement and reassurance. At the last goodbye, my stomach somersaulted, and I began to regret eating so much food.

Lieutenant Marshall was the last to arrive. He held a white watch with a blue screen between his thumb and forefinger. He held it out to me.

"This, Mia, will be your lifeline on Usonia. It's been preloaded with all of your personal information. It will unlock your home, your car... It's how you access the public transport system and your school... It's also how you pay for things on Usonia... It's connected to your great grandfather's bank account, so don't go wild." He smiled at the look on my face. "We also pre-entered all the biological information from your tests in here. The watch will constantly measure your pulse and blood pressure, and it even keeps tabs on your daily steps. Now this is very important," he said sternly. "To activate the watch, you need to place your right thumb on the screen. It will only respond to *your* thumb print. If you ever take it off, you *must* make sure you deactivate it first, in exactly the same way. This is the most valuable piece of equipment you will ever have in your possession."

He waited for me to strap the watch to my wrist and then I gingerly pressed my thumb to the screen. It lit up and a welcome message glided across the screen.

Then the lieutenant picked up my suitcase and gestured for me to follow him. I must have looked like a lamb being led to the slaughter. I had an overwhelming desire to run back and lock myself in my cell, but I carried on regardless. The lieutenant looked back and smiled encouragingly.

"This is an amazing opportunity, Mia, I know it doesn't seem that way right now. Promise me you'll savour every moment, and won't waste each precious second wishing you were somewhere else."

I nodded vigorously but didn't want to risk speaking in case my voice broke. I followed the lieutenant into a circular, windowless chamber and gasped. A platform ran alongside the circumference of the room and a sort of gangplank led from near where I was standing into the centre of the room. In the middle, sat a large pewter-coloured ship. A ring circled its middle, blue lights decorating the rim and pulsing softly, as if on standby. I was in awe. It looked nothing like any of the NASA spaceships I'd seen on TV. In fact, it looked like nothing I'd ever seen before, except, except... I didn't want to admit it, even to myself, but it looked.... It looked virtually identical to every image of a flying saucer that I'd seen - and discounted as nonsense - throughout my *entire* life. I was literally speechless and found myself turning to the lieutenant, wide eyed with wonder.

"You have *got* to be kidding... UFOs have been government spaceships all along?"

Lieutenant Marshall let out a deep belly laugh. "That's right, Miss McAdams... There is, in fact, no other intelligent life in the universe. We just go on letting people think that the big cover up is to do with aliens, but we know they don't exist. We don't want anyone finding out about Usonia until it's ready for mass inhabitation. It's a big job building a sustainable planet that can house the entire population of Earth..."

"Wow... So, all UFO sightings, ever, have actually been you guys? Even that big conspiracy theory about aliens crash-landing in... was it Roswell?"

"That's right. It was the 7th of July 1947 - a tragic day for the mission." The lieutenant's expression turned suddenly serious. "The prototype spaceship was a catastrophic failure. The ship crashed on its return to land near Roswell, New Mexico, killing the captain and the skeleton crew on board. The disaster was quickly covered up as an intelligence mission against the USSR, but the local alien conspiracy theorists didn't hurt our cause."

"That's awful." I clasped my hand over my mouth.

"It was a dark day for Project Ark. But, the second launch was a success, and a little over two years later, humans first inhabited the planet Usonia." The lieutenant smiled then. "And that, Miss, is where you're headed. Now stop stalling and let's get you on that spaceship."

Suddenly, it felt like there was a hamster running around my stomach in one of those little plastic balls. I could feel my heart thumping quickly and loudly in my chest. This was it. I was actually leaving planet Earth and going into space. I swallowed loudly and then followed Lieutenant Marshall, who was waiting patiently at the foot of the gang plank. My foot steps on the metal walkway echoed around the chamber, bouncing off the panelled walls and metal fabric of the spaceship.

Inside, was a maze-like mess of white padded tubes, all either leading to, or circling a central communal space. The lieutenant lead me to one of the rooms wrapping the communal area. He swiped his wrist at the door and it snapped open, revealing a tiny pod containing a raised bed that was set into the wall. An internal door led to the most compact bathroom I'd ever seen. The lieutenant swiped his wrist again and a door opened beneath the bed. He placed my belongings inside and then ushered me back out into the hallway. He pointed to various doors. Many led to storage, used mostly for mail and any other crucial supplies for the planet. Others housed the kitchen, a gym, cinema and playroom. Back in the centre of the ship, a spiral staircase dominated the middle of the room. I followed the lieutenant up the stairs and found myself encased in a large glass dome. In front sat two chairs, facing outwards and surrounded by controls, panels of buttons, screens and flashing lights. A man and woman turned and stood to greet us with wide smiles.

"You must be Mia." The woman grinned, holding out her hand. "My name's Pamela. I'll be your captain for this trip, and this is my second in command, Dylan."

Dylan reached out to shake my hand. "It's such a pleasure to meet you. I'm a big fan of your great grandfather's." He smiled widely.

"Get yourself settled in while we fire this baby up. You're in for a long ride!" Pamela drawled and moved back towards the control panel.

The lieutenant led me to a reclining chair to the left of the glass dome. He talked me through the complicated belt system that fixed me into the recliner and then stood back.

"This is an experience of a lifetime, Mia. Usonia is going to blow you away."

With a short wave, he was gone. The doors closed behind him and a low rumble started beneath me. I felt the ship disengage from the dock and we began to drift upwards. I didn't have time to question anything that was happening; we were moving so quickly that my brain seemed to be playing catch up. Before I knew it, we'd shot through the roof and were hurtling through the sky.

I was propelled backwards and into my seat as the ship accelerated, climbing steadily away from Earth and towards the misty threshold of the atmosphere. Through the dome, I watched as the sky around us dimmed from the bright blue of the New Mexico sky, through a spectrum of colour, to a black so devoid of light that, for the first time, I truly understood what the word 'nothing' really meant.

The invisible force that was pinning me to my seat all of a sudden shifted, and the ship became eerily silent. I started to feel strangely light; weightless, as if I were a helium balloon. My body seemed to take on a life of its own and began to drift away from the recliner, straining at the straps that held me in place.

The ship tilted then and altered its course. What came into view next left me dumbstruck. For the first time, words that I'd used liberally and without conviction throughout my entire life, actually applied. Words like awesome, incredible, wonderful... all took on a new and gut-wrenching meaning. No words existed that could do this sight justice. The sight of your own planet, an image almost as familiar as your own face, shrinking away from you and disappearing into the distance. A tiny globe, small enough to fit inside a doll's house. My eyes welled up with water and I was filled with a blurred mix of pain and sorrow and pride.

Before long, the atmosphere in the cabin changed again. The world around me seemed to turn to normal; the lightness replaced with a new-found awareness of gravity. The captain's voice drifted from the speakers, announcing that artificial gravity had been switched on, and I was free to roam around the ship.

I snapped open the seat belts, extricated myself from the straps and then clambered out of my seat. Pamela and Dylan looked deep in concentration, so I decided to slip off and explore my new temporary abode. I ventured down the stairs and circled the ship, poking my head into all of the rooms and storage spaces that my new watch would allow me to access. I played around in the gym for a little while, trying out various weight machines and testing the cardio equipment. Feeling like I'd exerted myself enough for one day, I wandered into the kitchen and rummaged in the draws for snacks, but none of the space food looked in the least appealing. I'd just started to head back towards the control deck when I bumped into Dylan as he came down the stairs.

"Here you are…" He smiled. "I was just coming to

look for you. I'm on a break now - keep me company?"

"I'd love to," I said, relieved to have some human contact. I wasn't good at entertaining myself for extended periods of time.

"Great, follow me." He set off towards the playroom, picking up some fruit on his way past the kitchen. We stepped into the room and instantly we began drifting upwards.

Dylan floated off ahead and then spun back and called from the other side of the room, "Hey, watch this, Mia."

I turned to look and watched as he let go of each piece of fruit in turn, and began to juggle in slow motion.

"Here, you try." He knocked the apples and oranges slowly in my direction and I grabbed them one by one.

I started to throw the fruit up in the air warily. I usually tried to avoid all kinds of ball games, sports, and physical activity in general. I was blessed with zero athletic ability and detested taking part in things I wasn't any good at. But I caught the fruit with ease and found myself actually juggling. It was like magic. I felt like I could conquer almost anything in that room. A smile involuntarily spread across my face.

"Open wide," Dylan said, releasing a chocolate-coated peanut from his hand. I drifted towards it and snapped my mouth shut around the ball of chocolate.

"Hungry?" he asked, spinning another one in my direction.

I nodded vigorously and caught it before it floated out of reach.

"Let's go eat some real food. And when I say 'real' food, please be advised I'm using that term very loosely." He performed a backflip in the air and then swam towards the door.

I followed Dylan into the kitchen and watched as he slid the selection of ready meals out of the locked drawer.

"What do you feel like? We've got pasta, pasta, oh, and more pasta."

"Lucky I like pasta." I was so hungry that I'd have eaten anything by that point. I don't think I'd ever been so active before landing in New Mexico.

Pamela joined us just as Dylan was placing three steaming hot bowls of pasta on the table.

"Wait a minute... If you're here, and I'm here... Who's flying this ship?" Dylan asked, looking from Pamela to me in mock concern.

Pamela rolled her eyes and looked at me reassuringly. "It's on autopilot, don't worry. We'll be ok for a few minutes while we eat."

Dylan sat down, wiping his brow in relief, and then speared three pieces of tortellini with his fork. "So, Mia, d'ya have a boyfriend?" he asked, a mouth full of food.

Pamela looked at him in horror. "Dylan... did you just think, 'Hey, what's the most embarrassing question I could ask a girl I only just met?'"

He grinned and shrugged.

"He doesn't get out much, I'm sorry." Pamela said, exchanging a look with me.

"No, it's ok…" I blushed. "I don't have a boyfriend. There was a guy at school, Jack, that I thought maybe could have been… But, well, now I'm here. And he's there. So that's all over now…" I didn't want to have to think about everyone I'd just had to leave behind; it was too painful. I changed the subject quickly. "What about you? Are you a couple?"

"God, no," Pamela said instantly, almost spitting out her food.

"Thanks, Pam, thanks a lot." Dylan clutched his chest as if she'd caused him physical pain.

"I'm sorry, Dylan, no offence intended. No, we're both single… It's pretty impossible to hold down a relationship with this job. All the dishonesty, the time away…"

"Yeah, it's not so much the lying and travelling that I have the problem with," Dylan started.

"Of course you'd say that," Pamela said rolling her eyes.

"It's more the fact that all women think that I'm a complete loser."

I caught Pamela's eye and could see her struggling to stifle a laugh.

"I can't tell anyone how cool my job actually is, you know? All my friends just think I'm a failed astronaut, working an admin job at the base until I get clearance to go into space, which might never happen. If people knew what I really did, that I get to fly a spaceship to another planet every two weeks…"

Pamela cleared her throat and Dylan looked at her questioningly.

"Well, technically *I* fly this ship," she said.

"That's beside the point."

"Is it though?" she said shaking her head.

"My *point* being, that if I could tell the truth about my job, I'd have girls hanging off my every word."

Pamela laughed, "Ok, Dylan, whatever you say… Personally, I just think it wouldn't be fair to start a relationship. You'd have to leave your partner for a week at a time… and it would be impossible to start a family. I couldn't do that to my children. To my family."

My own parents came to mind then and I thought Pamela probably had a point.

I quickly pushed them out of my thoughts and started to clear the table.

"Well, no rest for the wicked," Pamela said, standing up. "We'd better get back to flying this ship… Rest up, Mia, we'll see you in the morning. G'night honey."

I spent the remainder of the three-day journey either sleeping, eating, watching movies, or performing amateur acrobatics in the Zero G playroom. Dylan and Pamela kept me company whenever they took a break and that became the highlight of each day. I think I'd have gone crazy if I didn't have them to talk to throughout the trip.

I was just starting to feel at home on the ship when

Pamela announced that we were about to descend on Usonia and needed to return to our seats for re-entry. My stomach back-flipped and a stab of terror seared right through my middle. I was about to step foot onto another planet, in an entirely different solar system. My world would quite literally never be the same again.

Strapped into the reclining seat, I felt the ship begin to decelerate sharply as we approached a new and unfamiliar sphere, encased in a thick, fog-like substance. Beyond the haze, the globe was decorated with a mosaic of sapphire, emerald and amber. The planet glittered like a jewel in the moonlight. I was mesmerised.

I felt a strong force take over the interior of the ship and I was once again pushed back into my chair, as the ship drove its way through the dense, viscous atmosphere. We descended quickly and almost soundlessly, landing seemingly effortlessly.

Pamela turned to me cheerfully. "This is your stop, Miss McAdams!"

I weakly returned her smile and fumbled with the seat belt. My hands were shaking and a dull tingle spread across my skin. My breath had become short and I found myself gulping fruitlessly for air. I eventually managed to disengage myself from the chair and stood up quickly. Filling my lungs with oxygen, I steeled myself for what was next.

Chapter 4

I turned to make my way towards the central staircase just as a woman appeared at the top. She must have been about seven feet tall, with long tanned limbs and a mane of thick, glossy, flaxen hair. She smiled and I was almost blinded by the dazzle from her perfect white teeth. She looked like an oversized Barbie doll. She strode over like a super model, grabbed me by the shoulders and kissed me on both cheeks.

"Mia!" She beamed. "We're all so thrilled you're here. How was your flight? Are you well rested? You must be absolutely starving... Let's get your things. You must be excited to be here. Are you nervous? Of course you are, darling, of course you are. You poor thing."

The Barbie doll babbled for some time, without pausing for breath, let alone for my responses, and then she stopped suddenly. She threw her head back and burst into melodic laughter. "Goodness! With all the excitement, I don't think I've even introduced myself… Have I? Do you know who I am darling?"

My mouth opened and closed, waiting for a gap in her monologue of rhetorical questions.

"Of course you don't, dear. How could you?! Let me introduce myself." She stopped, inhaled briefly, and then held out her long, slender hand. "I'm Priscilla. I work with your great grandfather at The Administration. He asked me to pick you up today. I hope you don't mind. You look a little bewildered, I'm confusing you aren't I?! Gosh, we're just over the moon to have you here! Follow me, I'll help you with your things."

Pamela and Dylan laughed quietly, shaking their heads, and moved over to join us. They both wrapped their arms tightly around me, before waving us off, shouting their goodbyes and well wishes. I followed Priscilla down the steps, enviously admiring her slender hourglass figure, encased in a simple cotton wrap dress. She picked up my bags, and strode off the ship, still prattling on without seeming to need any answers. It was vaguely reassuring since I hadn't quite gathered my thoughts well enough to speak.

We emerged into a tall, white, roofless room. I looked up to see the bluest sky I had ever seen, or could even have imagined. It was a blue that was so deep and so bright that it was almost the colour of cyan ink.

Priscilla marched forwards, leading me into a light and bustling transport hub. As I skipped to catch up, she turned back to provide a running commentary. "This is Usonia's core transport interchange, but people refer to it as the Citi. This part is where we Usonians come for intraplanetary travel. Instead of using planes like you do on Earth, we use spaceships for long distance travel. They're much more simple than the ship you arrived on, of course, darling. Travel anywhere on the planet takes under an hour, so they're built more like round versions of your trains."

I looked around the large circular room. A clear dome formed the ceiling, showing off the aqua sky. All around me, queues of beautiful, Amazonian-like people formed in front of gang planks that led to compact space shuttles.

Clear doors snapped open beneath a sign that read 'Hyper Transport System' and we entered another large, white spherical room.

"We're very lucky on Usonia. The first settlers found two natural renewable resources, soon after they landed. The first, they called neige. It's the glittering white material you see all around you. It looks like snow doesn't it?" She swept her arm around the room and turned to me smiling. I nodded in agreement, transfixed. "It's like a hybrid of stone and glass, so it almost has the look and feel of a high gloss plastic, but it's totally natural and as renewable as the wood from the trees." She stopped then and pointed to the ceiling. "The second is this clear material you see. It's essentially glass, and we call it that, but it's lighter, safer and more durable. It's made from a sand-like substance that renews a million times quicker than the sand on Earth."

Priscilla moved quickly off again and headed towards a circular entranceway on the left hand side of the main hall. It was labelled Paramount City. She swiped her watch at the entry point and then turned to check that I had done the same. We were moving so fast that I had no time to process any thoughts, I just focused on not being left behind.

We sat down in a two-seater vehicle, a bit like an engineless car, but curved and made partially from the white material they called neige, roofed with a dome - obviously. They definitely liked their glass domes here on Usonia. This must be what happens when you have one designer create a whole planet back in the 1950s. It was kind of cool in a retro-futuristic way.

We sat back into the cotton seats and I looked around for a seat belt. Priscilla laughed. "There are no seatbelts here, dear; the transport system is 100% safe."

I doubted that really, but I was in no position to argue. The car suddenly began to descend in a perfectly straight, vertical direction, like a really smooth, fast elevator, and I held onto the seat automatically.

Priscilla laughed again and shook her head at me. "I guess it'll take some getting used to…"

The car stopped after a few moments and we sat hovering in front of another glass doorway that led to a long white tube. The red light glowing above the entrance flicked to green and we were propelled back into our seats.

I turned to Priscilla, "This is unreal!"

"They're the first words you've uttered all morning," she said laughing. "We don't know any different, of course, but I've heard about your transport modes on Earth. They sound awful!"

I nodded in agreement.

"Apart from intra and interplanetary travel, our entire transport system is housed beneath the surface of the planet. We have an underground tube network that's run on magnets. Usonia is the most magnetic planet in the universe and we harness that energy to power the capsules. We're travelling at 1200km an hour right now, can you believe it?"

"That is so cool..." I breathed. Cool was clearly a massive understatement but I was so overwhelmed by this amazing new world that no better word came to mind.

"The system generates no pollution, and because it's underground, the whole of Usonia is pedestrianised, making it the safest place in the universe. The main central line only travels in one direction so there's no risk of traffic accidents, but even so, all the capsules are made from magnets, so if one came into contact with another capsule, they would repel each other. Any power that the system needs to run comes from the planet's underground thermal energy source, and all the planet's services - you know - pipes, cables, etcetera - are all connected to the tubing, so we don't need to dig up the ground every time something needs to be fixed. We take it for granted of course, but I've heard that's not how it works on Earth. How could you bear it?"

"Well, we don't know anything else… It's just reality for us, I suppose." It occurred to me then how different we were to the Usonians. How readily we accepted terrible conditions as normal and did little or nothing to change it, while they took the complete opposite for granted.

The capsule slowed quickly to a stop, hovered for a second and then zipped upwards, towards the light.

We came to a stop in what I suppose we would call a garage, but it wasn't one of the ramshackle storage sheds that I was used to; it was pristine and sparkling and light. The door to the capsule swung open and Priscilla led the way, pulling my luggage behind her. She swiped us both through a door with her watch and we entered a room that I could only describe as palatial. I'd never really felt deprived as a child. I came from middle class parents and I lived in a big home in a really lovely part of town. But this was something else. Triple height ceilings, floor to ceiling windows, walnut floors, domed roof lights… I wanted to run around and bounce on the furniture. I walked around the room with my mouth wide open, touching everything I passed. I ran my fingers across the linen upholstered oak furniture, stroking a cashmere throw and then sat down, hugging a silk cushion to myself.

I turned to Priscilla, who was stood in the doorway, smiling at my reaction. "I can't believe how luxurious everything is! I knew my great grandfather was some kind of celebrity but I had no idea he lived like a king! This is insane."

Priscilla laughed. "Actually, we all live this way. We try to live equally and naturally on Usonia. Everything you see here is natural, renewable, friendly to our environment, and built to last so that we minimise waste."

"Seriously? So everyone here lives in some kind of palace?"

"Well, yes… Only, again, it's just normal for us. I forget how cramped and ugly the living conditions mostly are on Earth. It's so refreshing seeing everything through your eyes. Of course, we all love living here. We're a happy, peaceful race and have very little to complain about. Come on darling, let me show you to your room."

Priscilla picked up my bags and led me through a solid oak doorway to a spacious curved room. It was like being in the turret of a castle - I felt like a Disney princess. A large bed sat in the centre of the sunny room and faced a glazed wall overlooking a garden filled with lush green plants and brightly coloured flowers. Priscilla moved towards a door on the right hand side of the room and gestured for me to follow her. The doorway led to a walk-in wardrobe that was the size of my entire bedroom at home. It was lined with rails and shelves and hooks, all teeming with the most beautiful clothes and accessories.

"Your great grandfather asked me to pick up some things for you, I hope they're ok..?"

"Ok?! They're the most amazing clothes I have

ever seen. Literally." I walked through the wardrobe in a daze, fingering cashmere sweaters, linen one-pieces and silk dresses. I felt like I'd won the lottery, only I didn't even have to buy the ticket.

"Well, I suppose you must be exhausted, my poor dear. I need to get back to The Administration, but I'll leave you here to rest, unpack and get settled before Herb finishes work. He can't wait to meet you, Mia. You're the only family he has, you know? He's so happy you decided to come."

Priscilla gave me a little hug and then left the room in a flash of gold and bronze. I lay back on the bed and just stared dazedly at my surroundings. Priscilla was right, I was exhausted. I felt like I was in some kind of blissful dream and I didn't want to wake up.

I had just a few hours before I was going to meet the great Herbert McAdams for the first time. He seemed to be famous on this planet, I suppose being the last remaining founding father. He must be about a hundred years old by now. My mother had barely mentioned him so I had no idea what to expect and I was a little nervous about meeting this grand political figure - my great grandfather or not. I hurried to freshen up and change into some of my new clothes, eager to make a good first impression.

Chapter 5

After a rejuvenating bubble bath in my luxurious ensuite bathroom, I'd wrapped my hair into a knot and thrown on a mushroom-coloured linen shift dress. I sat nervously in the living room, alternating between sitting, standing and pacing, fidgeting with my ears or the hem of my dress.

I was seated awkwardly on the edge of a bamboo chair when Herbert McAdams walked into the room. I dropped my hands into my lap and leapt up nervously. A man that looked like a movie star from the 1950s strode into the room wearing a cream linen suit and a fedora hat. He reminded me a little of images I'd seen of Humphrey Bogart or Frank Sinatra. He was tall and strong-looking with a shock of silvery white hair and a sort of natural elegance and presence that I'd never come across in real life.

He hung up his hat and was just wrapping a brown

silk scarf around the coat stand when he noticed me. His face creased into a wide smile and his eyes sparkled, "Well now, young lady! You must be the much anticipated Miss Mia McAdams!" He moved quickly across the room and clutched my shoulders with both hands. He kissed me on each cheek and then stepped back without releasing his grip. He peered at me with what looked like delight. "You look just like Mary. That's your grandmother, my late daughter, of course. An Earthling like you… The resemblance is uncanny, really. It's only those eyes that set you apart… Like a stormy sea." His hands dropped to his sides and he shook his head, chuckling, but without taking his eyes off me. "So much to catch up on! Let me freshen up and I'll be right back with you. Please do take a seat at the dining table, and make yourself at home."

My evening with Herbert McAdams was a genuine pleasure. I'd never experienced being with an elderly person who was so engaging and interesting. He didn't just talk about himself and his accomplishments, while complaining about the youth of today and the world we now live in. He was actively interested in my life on Earth and was full of stories of his time there and our family. It felt like he was an old friend - familiar and warm. I'd quickly decided to name him GG, as Great Grandfather seemed cumbersome and formal, the complete opposite of this man sat before me.

"How old are you, GG, do you mind me asking?" I said as I spooned a blend of berries and honey into my mouth.

"I'm 95 years old, almost to the day! And fit as a fiddle." He beamed at me, his eyes twinkling. I inspected his radiant skin, flushed with health, and his bright knowing eyes. He really did look the picture of health.

"What's your secret? I wouldn't have been surprised if you'd said you were 55," I said seriously.

He chuckled. "It's no secret. It's just life here on Usonia. We have an exceptional life expectancy on this planet. We have no pollution, a healthy outdoorsy lifestyle, our diets are natural and nutritious and we lead a near perfectly stress-free existence. The transport system we have here has ended traffic accidents and we are blessed with a thicker ozone layer which protects us from the sun. Usonians don't smoke or drink, combine that with an incredibly mixed gene pool, and we have the healthiest race that ever existed. Of course, I wasn't born here, so my life expectancy will naturally be lower, but most Usonians will live well into their hundreds." He put down his spoon, and looked at his watch. "Goodness, is that the time! It's your first day at school tomorrow, Mia, you'd better get an early night. I'll walk you there in the morning and help get you enrolled."

I was surprised to find that I fell quickly into a peaceful and deep sleep. I'd imagined that I'd have a restless night, full of dreams of missing my alarm or turning up to school in my underwear. The combination of three days of travelling and the complete overload of information I'd received that day must have really knocked it out of me. I was awoken gradually and naturally by the sunlight that streamed through the roof lights, and the sociable chirruping of birds hopping from tree to tree outside my window. I felt strangely relaxed and calm. And then I remembered that I had to start school that day, and my stomach turned.

Starting school anywhere new is a fairly daunting experience. Starting a new school on another planet is, well, terrifying. Especially when everyone at your school is like a super human being.

I pulled on a grey cotton sundress and then stood in front of the mirror, analysing my face dejectedly. I prodded at skin so pale that it was almost transparent. An uneven splash of freckles dusted my long straight nose and I critically studied the slight gap in between my two front teeth. My eyes scanned my reflection, passing over thin lips, grey eyes, and limp mousy hair… I was going to stand out like a sore thumb. My stomach somersaulted at the sound of GG calling my name. I gave my hair a shake in a pointless attempt to generate some volume and then reluctantly made my way towards the door.

"Good morning, Darling!" GG boomed cheerfully. "You look just wonderful – so well rested! The image of a true English rose… How did you sleep, dear?"

"Surprisingly well… That bed is so comfortable; it was a struggle convincing myself to leave it."

"And how are you feeling? Nervous?" GG collected his hat and scarf from the coat rack and opened the door, waiting for me to exit, before pulling the door behind us.

"Terrified. I feel a bit sick." I put my hand on my stomach to ease the churning.

"You'll be fine, dear, I promise you. Teenagers on Usonia aren't the same as on Earth. Usonians are a warm and friendly bunch."

I thought back to every Usonian I'd met so far, and he was right. They were all excessively pleasant. Hopefully that applied to teenagers too.

We stepped outside to a perfect summer's day. A warm breeze ruffled the trees and the sun shimmered in the bright blue sky.

"Are the seasons the same here?" I asked, suddenly conscious of how little I knew about my new home.

"It's most like California, I suppose. There's little seasonal change, and the weather is agreeable throughout the year. We've positioned all settlements along the equator so daylight hours are consistent and all cities benefit from similar, temperate climates."

I turned back towards the house, having gradually become aware that we hadn't gone in the direction of the garage. "We're not taking the car?"

GG laughed. "We call them caps here, short for capsule. But no, we'll walk. All the cities have been designed around central social hubs and everywhere is pedestrianised, so we tend to use our legs as transport from day to day." He winked and marched on ahead.

I hurried to catch up but found myself too easily distracted by the scenery. Various pathways had been created using either timber boards or cobbled stone, leading the way to the centre. All around were flowering trees: soft pink cherry blossoms, violet jacaranda trees and jasmine bushes that smelled good enough to eat. It was eerily strange to be in a place completely devoid of cars and buses. No ugly heaps of metal cluttering the environment, no exhaust fumes polluting our lungs, no rumbling engines masking the sound of bird song and the breeze in the trees. I inhaled, filling my lungs with oxygen, and felt the corners of my mouth turn upwards; a smile unconsciously creeping across my face.

After a short walk, we arrived at my new school. It seemed more modern than the rest of Usonia that I'd seen so far. From a distance, I could see a curved, semi circular building made from a light-coloured timber. It faced onto a courtyard filled with trees, and benches that were peppered with children that could easily have stepped off a catwalk.

As we walked up the stone path towards the school entrance, I suddenly felt incredibly tiny. Gargantuan specimens walked by, swinging their manes of hair, laughing and chattering and jostling with each other. I was considered fairly small on Earth at five feet three inches, but here I was actually tiny. I was even shorter than most of the younger children.

I was mesmerised by the people surrounding me. Their skin was so rich, glowing and luminous that it seemed as if it were actually metallic. Their eyes were huge, wide-set and sparkling. Their teeth bright and perfectly straight. Their hair was thick, glossy and in vibrant colours. I realise I am starting to make these people sound like thoroughbred horses, but then I suppose that's what they were – a pure breed, super human race.

GG noticed my slack-jawed, wide-eyed stare and smiled. "Usonians are a good-looking bunch aren't they?" I nodded in vigorous agreement. "They're a perfect cross-breed of the entire population of Earth. All the colours of the world combined to create a rich, deep golden skin tone. Of course, it helps that they're a naturally healthy race – they eat nutritious food and are active for fun. They spend time in the sunshine and are relaxed and happy. All of these elements combine to make an enviously attractive race."

GG led the way to the school reception area and we were greeted, as seemed to be the standard on Usonia, with generous smiles of welcome. GG completed all the necessary paperwork while I skim-read my lesson plan. I seemed to have only one teacher who would be taking all of my classes - a Mr Kepler. I barely recognised any of the subjects from my previous school. Maths, Science, History and English were familiar, but from there, it was perfectly clear that this was a school in another world. My classes included nutrition, ethics, sustainability, international relations, practical studies, active studies and astronomy, along with politics and computing. Add to that an overabundance of language lessons, from Mandarin and Hindi to Spanish, Russian and Arabic, and I was going to be in way over my head.

"Why so many language classes?" I asked GG, looking up worriedly from my lesson plan.

"Well, you know that English is the language used by Usonians, of course. But you see, we're preparing to populate the planet with the people of Earth at some point in the future. So, to make that as harmonious as possible, we encourage all Usonians to learn at least the basics in the major languages used on Earth."

GG looked at his watch. "I'd better get off to The Administration. And you, my dear, are going to be late to your first class if you don't hurry." He kissed me on both cheeks, tipped his hat to the receptionist who practically curtseyed in response, and then he disappeared through the glass doors. Before I had time to gather my thoughts, a dazzling copper-haired, bronzed creature appeared in front of me, almost blinding me with her smile. She was willowy and ungainly, almost as if her limbs were new appendages and she hadn't quite yet worked out how to control them. She held out a slender hand and smiled delightedly. "You must be Mia! My name is Stella. I've been assigned as your buddy to help you settle into the school."

I took her hand, relieved that I wasn't going to be left to navigate the corridors alone, and smiled back.

"We're going to be late, darling, so we'd better run. Follow me!" Her lithe figure sped off in front of me and I had to skip to catch up. I was going to have to get used to walking fast on this planet with my short legs. Stella stopped abruptly in front of a timber door and I almost crashed into her. "Oops, sorry." She giggled and then put a finger to her mouth. "Shhh." She slowly opened the door and peered inside.

"Ahhh, Stella, you've decided to join us at last; what a pleasure. Do come in!" A handsome, dark-haired man in his 40s called out from the desk with a cheery smile. "And you've brought a guest! How lovely. I suppose you must be the infamous Mia McAdams. Come in, come in." He gestured wildly with his arms.

I crept shyly into the room while Stella snuck to the back and slid into her seat.

"Well, class, we have a very special new student... Mia is the Great Granddaughter of our last remaining founding father, Herbert McAdams. I'm sure you'll all make her feel very welcome!" The class broke into excited murmurs and Mr Kepler quickly hushed everyone. "Take a seat at the back, Mia, next to Stella over there." He smiled encouragingly and I moved quickly and quietly towards my seat.

"Perfect timing, Mia, you've joined us for one of my favourite history lessons... The history of our planet, Usonia. You're in for a treat."

I looked around and noticed the whole class lean in eagerly to listen to his words – the polar opposite to any classroom I'd been in to date. I was scanning the room with interest when a boy caught my attention. He wasn't leaning forward enthusiastically like the others, rather he was sat back in his chair reticently. Watching Mr Kepler without expression, quietly and reservedly listening, taking in every word, almost as if it were oxygen. I was staring at this boy without thinking, when his eyes flicked to meet mine. Our eyes locked and I was spellbound for a moment, held mesmerised by his startling golden brown eyes. Then he was staring straight ahead again and my cheeks grew hot at having been caught out. I sat up in my seat and gathered all of my will to resist temptation and focus my attention on Mr Kepler and the history lesson.

Chapter 6

"I'm going to take you back now, class... Right back to the days before Usonia was even a twinkle in someone's eye." Mr Kepler paced around the classroom as he spoke. "All the way back to 1945. World War II was coming to an end and nuclear testing was just beginning." He pressed some buttons on a key pad and images suddenly appeared on the wall behind him. At the same time, the transparent desks in front of all of us came to life, mirroring the images seen behind Mr Kepler. Sounds of missiles exploding reverberated around the room.

"Mia, the desk in front of you is an integrated, interactive touch screen computer. It will mirror what you see behind me, unless you use the touch screen facility to zoom in or navigate around the screen." I gingerly touched the glass and it followed my finger, sliding across to reveal more images and videos of missile testing during World War II.

"Now class, can anyone tell me when the first atomic bomb was dropped in warfare?" A sea of hands shot straight up and I slunk into my seat embarrassed that I hadn't the faintest idea. I peered to my left and caught sight of the boy I'd noticed at the start of the lesson. He was staring ahead, quietly confident, but wasn't fighting with the rest of the class to be picked.

"Ah, Noah. Since you're the only Usonian who hasn't raised their hand, perhaps you'd like to tell Mia the answer to this question?"

He turned to me and I flushed, looking quickly down at my screen, desperate to avoid eye contact. His voice came out strong and clear, but I couldn't see the expression on his face. "It was on the 6th of August, 1945."

"Very good, Noah, very good. The first atomic bomb used in warfare was dropped by the US, on the Japanese city of Hiroshima. The second world war ended less than a month afterwards, and in October that same year, 51 world states formed to become the United Nations. And this is where our histories take different paths, Mia. For one of the first, little known, tasks that the leaders convened to tackle, was the preservation of the human race, under the real threat of nuclear warfare. World leaders, from the US, Russia, Great Britain, China, India and France, united to formulate a protection strategy, which became known as Project Ark. The task force meticulously selected two adults from each of the 51 founding member states – the best of the best – the most athletic, intelligent, healthy, talented human beings, and they were sent to a secret training facility in New Mexico."

Black and white images flashed up on the screens, depicting images of lectures and boot camp style preparation.

"The team was installed at Holloman Airforce base, which was originally a British training facility during World War II. This elite task force went on to become our founding fathers – only one of whom remains." Mr Kepler paused and looked at me. "And that's your great grandfather, Mia."

The pictures on the screens switched abruptly to images of rockets and spaceships. I glanced to my right and watched Stella leaning over her screen, zooming in and out and flicking through the images and video footage, completely absorbed. I dared to peer to my left and from the corner of my eye, I could see Noah, still sat back in his seat, looking ahead and observing quietly.

"Using advanced German rocket technology captured by the US at the end of the war, the team began working on a classified prototype to allow interstellar travel. The prototype ship was test-launched on the 2nd of July 1947 but infamously crash landed near Roswell, tragically killing everyone on board. New recruits joined the team soon afterwards, and work began again in earnest. The mission had a major boost in 1949 when the military alliance NATO was formed. The project quickly gained the support of

NATO members, and with their financial backing, the plans soon became a reality. Spaceship Beta launched on the 1st of October 1949 and landed three days later on the planet we came to know as Usonia, the planet we now call home."

Images of the empty, unpopulated planet appeared on our screens. It was truly beautiful.

"Back on Earth, the world's leaders fought to cover up the mission, battling against frequent sightings of shuttles being sent back and forth with supplies for the settlers. The general public was in uproar over 'UFO' sightings and the threat of alien invasion. Of course we know now that there is no other intelligent life anywhere in the universe, which is why it is even more crucial that we preserve the human race.

"In the late 50s, the US began a very public space race with the USSR, serving as a distraction for the population of Earth. As part of this, in 1961, the first US specimen was publically sent into space. Can anyone tell me what that was?"

All hands shot up again, and I tentatively raised my hand. "Was it a chimpanzee?" I asked hesitantly.

Mr Kepler laughed. "That's right. A chimpanzee was sent into space from Holloman – the very airforce base from where our founding fathers began their journey, twelve years earlier. And the rest, as they say, is history! Does anyone have any questions?" Half of the class raised their hands as the bell rang. "Saved by the bell! Off you go kids, it's break time." I looked around, astonished, as my classmates reluctantly put their hands down and looked disappointed that the lesson was over. It was riveting for me because it was a complete reversal on everything I knew to be true. But surely everyone else had heard this a million times before.

"Isn't it the most amazing story?!" Stella gushed, linking her long, slender arm through mine and guiding me gently to the door, narrowly missing its frame.

I turned to Stella. "Weren't you bored out of your mind during that lesson?"

"Oh I just love the story of creation, I never tire of it… Don't you Earthlings have a story that you tell over and over again and it never gets old?" She looked at me expectantly, her rose-red mouth spread into an eager smile.

I thought for a minute, chewing at the corner of my lip. "There's the story of Christmas, I suppose."

"Christmas? Oh… how sweet! I remember studying your religions on Earth in history class. It's so alien for us to comprehend millions of people believing in so many conflicting, implausible ideas. And then fighting over them! We worship life on Usonia. Nature… The moon, the sun, the stars, the rivers…"

I stared at her in amazement. It was as if she were a hippy from the 1960s that had been cryogenically frozen and suddenly found herself in the 21st century. She wouldn't survive two minutes on Earth, but I needed a friend or two in this place and so I pasted a smile on my face and followed her out into the courtyard.

The rest of the day sped by in a blur. We had language classes in the afternoon but it wasn't as difficult as I'd been concerned about. We actually learned all the languages simultaneously, which I'd thought would be confusing, but it seemed to make more sense doing it that way. There was less repetition. I was partnered with Stella for the remainder of the day so she was on hand to help whenever I got lost, although Mr Kepler was extra patient and considerate, conscious that this was all completely new to me.

Stella walked me home at the end of the day and she chattered pleasantly along the way, pointing out landmarks and filling me in on innocent gossip about our neighbours. I'd had a surprisingly enjoyable day. GG was right, the teenagers really were excessively friendly here. I'd felt a little as if I'd been transported to Pleasantville at times. Their manner would probably have seemed false back at home, but it was clear they were being completely genuine.

I arrived home to an empty house and went straight to my room. I flopped onto the bed in a starfish shape and looked up at the darkening sky, decorated with emerging constellations of unfamiliar stars. I was finding life on Usonia unexpectedly tiring; there was so much new information to take in all of the time. I was looking forward to the point where life on this planet was just normal and I could finally be myself.

I heard the door open and close, signalling the return of my great grandfather. I reluctantly picked myself up off the bed and made my way into the living room. I painted a sunny expression on my face, but I was concerned to see GG wasn't his usual cheerful self. He looked up as I entered the room and his face quickly flicked from its morose countenance into something more approachable and jovial.

"Is everything ok, GG?"

"I hope so, darling, I truly hope so. We've had an incredibly frustrating day over at The Administration." He hung up his scarf and hat, frowning, and walked over to greet me. "I'm sure you don't want to hear me drivel on about politics all evening though; I wouldn't get me started if I were you, dear girl. Do tell me, how was your first day at Paramount High?"

I filled GG in on the events of the day over a cup of calming lavender and chamomile tea, before we moved into the kitchen to prepare dinner.

"Now, I suppose I'd better show you how this kitchen works so that you're capable of fending for yourself." GG led me to a large, complicated-looking piece of equipment in the centre of the room that looked something like a cross between a coffee machine and an all-purpose blender.

"You see these watches that we all wear?" He raised his wrist and nodded towards it. "They're all pre-programmed with every imaginable piece of information about each individual user – including your weight, height and any specific nutritional needs. This funny-looking machine that you're looking at now is in fact a high-tech intelligent cooker. You switch it on here and then enter the number of people you're cooking for. Then it asks for the first person to swipe their watch in front of the sensor, like so, go ahead, Mia."

I moved my wrist in front of the red light and the machine began processing my data. After a moment, it flashed up with different menu options for me to select from. I swiped through the available choices and then pressed select on a bean chilli with brown rice. It started to flash, indicating that it was ready to process the second diner's information. After GG went through the same process, the machine then began to list the ingredients required. Weighing scales and volumetric tubes were integrated above and beside the machine. We added raw ingredients one by one and the processer indicated when the correct quantities had been reached. Once we'd added all the ingredients, it whirred into action and began mixing and cooking the meals, flashing the estimated time remaining. When it was finished, we slid plates into the opening and our food was served.

"And there we have it!" GG proclaimed, collecting the dishes and delivering them to the table. "Two piping hot and perfectly balanced meals, tailored exactly to your body's nutritional needs. It's marvellous really, isn't it?"

We sat down and I took a tentative bite of the food. If I was at home, I would have point blank refused to eat anything healthy or nutritious, but I'd only just arrived and didn't want to offend GG, so I held myself back. But I was surprised to find it was delicious.

I had no idea you could eat healthy food that tasted good. Mum's idea of healthy was some lettuce leaves and a bottle of mineral water. I dug in, devouring the contents of the plate. After a few more mouthfuls, I pressed GG into telling me about his day. He sighed and put down his fork.

"We had a meeting with some government officials from Earth at The Administration this afternoon. These meetings usually all go the same way: We update the officials on our progress. They ask questions about delivery dates and targets. We confirm that we're on track to have the planet ready for mass inhabitation within the agreed ten year time period. And that's that. But there's an official that I've had doubts about for some time now. He doesn't usually speak up at these meetings, but it's always clear from his expression that he's disapproving in some way. Well, today he decided to make his concerns known. He told the room bluntly that the time we had been allowed was too generous. That there are vacant properties, towns and schools on this planet that are ready for inhabitation. He warned that sooner or later, people on Earth would get wind of Usonia's existence and there would be uproar. That we need to open up the boarders sooner." GG shook his head in anguish. "Of course our primary aim has always been to protect the longevity of the human race, but we were tasked with doing it the right way. Our aim as the founding fathers was to design, build and run a planet that is 100% sustainable, and I feel that somewhere along the line, the new world leaders have lost sight of that.

"The infrastructure of the planet isn't yet ready, neither are we capable of feeding and clothing the masses, without resorting to large scale, synthetic production, or depleting the planet's finite resources. And that goes against *all* of our values. He was adamant that we needed to speed up building by whatever means and I'm afraid to say the other officials began to side with him. Thankfully we've been given a reprieve until our meeting next fortnight, to allow us time to gather evidence and put a case forward for retaining the original migration date. But I'm worried. I've given almost my entire life to this mission. I came to this planet 65 years ago and now it seems like all of our hard work, quite literally our blood, sweat and tears, could all be undone and it would all have been futile. Something must be done to protect Usonia."

"That's terrible! If there's anything I can do…" I offered, concerned.

GG patted my shoulder and smiled sadly. "I'm not even sure there's anything *I* can do, my dear."

I'd only arrived on Usonia a few days ago, but already I was captivated. I imagined the beautiful landscape tarnished by ugly grey factories, the azure sky clouded with soot and smoke. It would be a travesty to spoil this planet because of the sheer impatience and ego of one overzealous government official. I was all for progress, but the Usonians were achieving just that. They were advancing as a race without causing detriment to the planet. I really wished there was something I could do to help, but I was just a teenager at school. If my great grandfather couldn't save Usonia, what could I do?

Chapter 7

The remainder of my first week at school felt as if it were over before it had really begun. I sat my first ecology, astronomy and sustainability lessons and was enthralled. There was so much to take in; it was fascinating.

I learned that the planet follows a different calendar and clock to Earth. Back in the '50s, one of the French founding fathers pioneered a metric, or decimal, system to account for time. There are ten days in each week and each day has only ten units of time, instead of 24. People sleep for three hours, work for four, and then relax and play for three. It took some getting used to.

Interplanetary post arrives every Friday night on Usonia and on Saturday morning, I awoke to receive my first letter from Earth. It was forwarded from my old home address and that seemed to make me happy and sad, all at the same time. I'd heard nothing from my mother, but maybe my being here was easier for her to deal with if she pretended I didn't exist any more. The letter contained a postcard from Spain showing a picture of a Flamenco dancer in an embroidered dress, clicking castanets next to man playing Spanish guitar. I turned it over to find a haphazardly scrawled note from my dad, apologising it was so late and explaining that, unsurprisingly, he'd forgotten to post it in Spain. The note continued onto a separate sheet of paper that I unfolded as I sat down to read it. It was a lengthy letter packed full of anecdotes about his Spanish escapades. He'd gotten food poisoning from a dubious paella joint on the harbour, and rescued a sack of abandoned kittens from a riverside, painstakingly finding them all new homes with the local Spaniards. He then went on to fall in and out of love with a flamenco dancer that looked just like the woman on the front of the card. My father seemed to live such a magical, fantastical life that I wondered how my mother had ever caught his attention in the first place. He was a free spirit of the truest kind.

It occurred to me at that moment that I might never see my father again. My eyes instantly filled with tears, but before the sobs could begin to escape, there was a tap at my door. I quickly rearranged my features, sniffed, and sat up on the bed. GG poked his head around the corner and looked pleased to see that I was up and dressed so early on a Saturday morning.

"Good morning, young Miss McAdams, I have a surprise visitor here for you." He pushed open the door to reveal a smiling, flame-haired Stella.

"Stella! What are you doing here? Not that it isn't a nice surprise." I smiled, pleased to see a friendly face. I stood up to welcome her and she gave me a big hug.

"Oh I just love your room! It's divine..." She twirled around in delight.

"Can I get you some tea, Stella?" GG asked pleasantly from the doorway.

"Oh thank you, Herb, but I won't take you up on the lovely offer. I've actually come to take Mia away. Show her some of the delightful sights of Usonia. What do you say, Mia?"

"That sounds amazing... Let me just grab my things."

"Yey!" She clapped. "Make sure you pack your swimsuit."

I stuffed everything I might possibly need into my canvas bag and threw it over my shoulder, kissing GG on the cheek as I passed.

"Have a wonderful day, girls!" GG held the door open for us and cheerfully waved goodbye.

Stella linked her arm through mine and then practically dragged me out of the house.

It was another incredibly beautiful day. The sun shone high in the sky and there wasn't a cloud in sight. The only sound was the twitter of birds in the trees and the wind rustling the leaves. It was so incredibly peaceful.

"Let's go to my place first. Have you eaten breakfast?" Stella asked while pulling me off to the right.

"No, I haven't, actually." With the excitement of the interplanetary post arriving overnight and then Stella appearing, I'd completely forgotten to eat.

"Great, I'm starving! Let's go and get breakfast."

After a short walk, we arrived at another grand, white house. The garden was full of exotic plants and trees. Palm trees stood on either side of the house like book ends. Tall bamboo waved and rustled in the breeze, fencing off the garden from the neighbours. And orchids and lilies decorated the cobbled path that led to the oak doorway.

We entered into a long bright corridor with large rooms shooting off from each side. Stella grabbed my hand and pulled me towards the kitchen.

"The house is shaped like a centipede. I absolutely love it! Because of the way it's designed, every room gets two full walls of windows. The south side of each room is the only exception because it's made completely from solar panels, so every room can generate its own power."

The kitchen was at the tail of the centipede and led onto a large, verdant garden, overflowing with vegetables and home-grown herbs. Chickens roamed freely, pecking at corn and flapping their useless wings.

Stella grabbed my hand and moved my wrist in front of the sensor on her oven.

"There you go. You can choose your breakfast now. I just need to go and collect the eggs from the hens, back in a sec."

I flicked through the menu and ended up with a breakfast of eggs, beans, tomato, spinach, mushroom and a sweet potato hash brown. It was beginning to dawn on me that there never seemed to be any meat in the menu options.

"Is everyone on Usonia vegetarian?" I asked Stella as she walked back into the room with her basket of eggs.

She laughed. "Not exactly." She put down the eggs and then selected her own breakfast. "There are no cows on the planet because they can be harmful to the atmosphere. We grow a lot of our own food so we mostly use that. We'll eat meat when an animal dies though. It's kind of a celebration. We have a big feast and eat every part of the animal for days, until we're completely sick of it."

She took our plates over to the big round table and we sat down to eat.

"Where are your parents?" I asked, suddenly noticing that the big house seemed very empty.

"Oh, they're probably at the market. All the farmers take their produce to market on a Saturday. It's held in the main square, I'll take you next week. We don't really have shops here so the market is the only place you can go to get things that you can't grow, make or print yourself."

"Print?"

"Yes, print." She looked at me as if I were from the dark ages. "I thought you had 3D printers on Earth?"

"I've heard about 3D printers, but normal people don't have them. It's more like a futuristic ideal."

"Then this. Is going. To change. Your life! Quick, finish up, let's go to the workshop."

The second I put down my knife and fork, Stella was dragging me out of my seat. She pulled me into a room that had a long work bench in the middle, with a giant printer on top and another large machine next to it. The wall behind it looked like some kind of twisted sweet shop. There were rows and rows of what looked like pic 'n' mix tubs, full of powders and shavings, all with scoops hanging next to them.

"Ok, come over here and watch some real life magic. Let's say... you need some new cutlery. You just browse through the designs on the screen here and then select the one you like and hit 'enter'. Then it will tell you the ingredients you need. It's just like the cooker." Stella led me over to the pic 'n' mix wall and began scooping up some filings that were labelled as silver. She poured them into a funnel at the top of the machine and then pressed 'enter' again. "You can buy the raw materials at the market, or you can recycle your own things."

The machine whirred around and flashed for a while and then it churned out a spoon. I stood there staring at it with my mouth wide open, speechless.

Stella laughed. "Go on; you can touch it."

I picked it up and spun it around in wonder. It was solid silver and perfect. Stella prised it from my hand and then beckoned me over to the second machine.

"This machine is what we use for recycling. It melts materials down, separates them, cools them and then turns them back into shavings or powders for us to use again. Cool, huh?"

"Amazing…" I was so impressed. I knew it was just a spoon, but it was more what that spoon represented. Earth just seemed so archaic in comparison to this planet.

Stella touched my arm suddenly. "Wait, you don't have a phone yet, do you?"

"Um, no, I didn't realise you had phones here?"

"We don't use them very often, but we do have them. I'll make you one. Come and pick the design you like. This one will take a little longer as there are more parts so it's a bit more complicated," Stella told me as she collected all the ingredients.

When it eventually popped out, she picked it up and then told me to follow her. We went back into the kitchen and she slid it into a holster on the window.

"It will just need to charge for a little while first. That's a solar-powered charger; it's really fast. We'll go out as soon as it's finished. Oh, and if you need the bathroom before we go, it's just down the hall. Don't get freaked out by the grey water in the toilet, it's just run-off from the sinks and showers."

"I noticed that at my great grandfather's. I just thought that must be the colour of the water here."

Stella laughed loudly. "The colour of the water here is crystal clear. Every building collects and filters its own water from the rain, but we don't like to waste anything, so we use recycled water to flush the toilet. Just don't be put off by the colour..." She gave me a little smile.

As we shut the door behind us, I realised we hadn't left a note for her parents. "Do your mum and dad know where we're going?"

Stella looked at me quizzically. "No... Why? Should they?"

"You mean you don't have to let your parents know where you are all the time?"

"Never, actually. Is that what you have to do on Earth?"

"Well, yes... In case we've been kidnapped or been hit by a car... They like to know when to expect us home so they don't have to worry, you know? And if we're not home on time, they know where to look for us."

Stella burst into laughter. "It really is a different world isn't it?! We all live very free and easy lives here. I'm lucky if I know where my parents are at any point. It's only because they're creatures of habit that I do. There's zero crime on this planet and there's also no alcohol, cigarettes, drugs... so parents have nothing to worry about. Usonians are all inherently good people. Plus, if anyone did anything bad, they would get shipped back to Earth. That's never happened, of course."

Stella skipped towards the outskirts of the town and in the direction of a dense, green forest. I had to run to catch up; she seemed to have boundless energy. I kept my head down and walked fast so that I didn't get left behind. I could feel beads of sweat forming on my brow. Too out of breath for words, we walked quickly and silently for what seemed like an eternity. Eventually, the trees began to thin out and we emerged at the edge of a cliff. I wiped my forehead and then collapsed on the ground panting, too exhausted to take in my surroundings. After a few moments, I opened one eye to see Stella bouncing up and down and laughing at me.

"Do you have cheerleaders on Usonia?" I asked, still grasping for oxygen.

"No... Why?"

"You'd be one if we were on Earth."

"Thank you!" She beamed.

"It wasn't a compliment." I closed my eye and tried to pretend she wasn't there.

"Come on; get up!"

I sighed loudly, and reluctantly clambered up, while Stella began peeling off her clothes. I fished in my bag for my swimsuit and then went to find a tree to hide behind.

"Earthlings are so strange," Stella said looking at me curiously.

"Turn around, I'm naked."

"We were all born naked, what's the big deal?"

"Maybe if I looked like you, it wouldn't be."

Stella shook her head in bemusement but turned her head to protect my modesty all the same.

I crept out from behind the tree and watched as Stella walked to the edge of the cliff. She turned back shouting, "Follow me!" and then star jumped into the void.

Chapter 8

I ran to the cliff edge in horror and arrived just as Stella plunged into a deep aqua pool. She emerged after a few seconds and wiped the water from her eyes. She blinked a few times and then smiled, calling, "Come and join me! The water's divine."

My stomach lurched at the thought, but I was really hot and sticky after the walk, and the water did look ludicrously inviting... I took a few steps back and then ran up to the edge. Holding my nose, closing my eyes and bundling myself up into a ball, I hurled myself off the cliff and landed seconds later with a splash. I resurfaced and pushed my hair off my face. I twirled around in the water and noticed my surroundings for the first time. To my left, a waterfall splashed and babbled, tumbling over amber-coloured rocks. A little further along, a small sandy cove curved around in a semi circle, water gently lapping at the shore. Pine trees lined the beach, stretching back, beyond where the eye could reach. At the edge of the beach, a steep rocky incline led back to the hill where we'd left our belongings. I looked down to see my toes wriggling beneath me. The water was so clear that I could see the sand metres below. Stella beckoned for me to follow her and then started to swim towards the shore.

We crawled out of the water and then lay flat on our backs, the water on our bodies glinting in the sunlight.

"I just love the way the sun feels on my skin; it's almost rejuvenating," Stella murmured, eyes closed and chin upturned towards the sun's rays. She reminded me of a beautiful, elegant lizard.

"Isn't this sun bad for you?" I asked, conscious that I didn't have any sun cream, and with my pale skin, I was terrified of burning.

"The planet is protected by a really thick ozone layer so it filters all the harmful rays before they reach us. It means we can enjoy the sun's light and warmth, and soak up the vitamin D without worrying about burning, aging or skin cancer."

"Is that because you haven't damaged your ozone layer with pollution?"

"We're not entirely sure. That's one theory. It's possible the layer surrounding Earth used to be thicker and more protective before the industrial revolution. Or perhaps Usonia is an evolved planet and the ozone layer grew thicker and more durable. We don't plan to test it though." She smiled at me then.

"How are you finding life on our planet, Mia?"

I shuffled around onto my front, took in the view before me and sighed. "It's the most beautiful place. So serene and calming. I've never been anywhere where everyone is so warm and welcoming. It's made leaving my friends and family a little easier." I felt my throat tighten as I thought of all the people I'd left behind.

"You must be missing your parents, I couldn't even imagine leaving mine." Stella propped herself up on one elbow. "Tell me about them."

I cleared my throat. "Well, my mum is pretty normal. I say normal, but I have no idea what normal is on this planet... She likes the simple things in life. A home-cooked meal, a glass of wine, a night in front of the television... She doesn't go out much and she's never travelled. Not until recently, anyway."

"And your dad?"

"He left when I was a little girl... I don't see him very often, but he writes to me all the time and we talk on the phone when we can. He travels a lot, so that makes it hard."

"What's he like?"

"He's the most generous person I know. I don't mean with money... He just always seems to be giving something of himself – his time, his energy... Whatever he has to give. He's always helping other people, or animals, even if it gets him into trouble. I remember him telling me that the two most important things in our society were equality and freedom, and we should never stop fighting for them."

"He sounds like a great man."

"He really is."

We lay there for a while longer, soaking up the sun. It was heavenly feeling the heat on my body, without the ominous tingle of burning skin.

I felt Stella fidget next to me. "I think that's enough vitamin D for one day. Let's go and wash off the sand. We should head off before it starts to rain."

I looked up at the sky but there wasn't a cloud to be seen. "How do you know it's going to rain?"

Stella dusted sand off the backs of her legs. "It rains at the same time every day here. You wouldn't have noticed at school. It mostly happens naturally because of the climate but sometimes they have to give the clouds a helping hand and blow them in the direction they're needed."

"You know exactly when it's going to rain? That's amazing…"

"Do you think so? It's kind of boring actually. How exciting it must be on Earth when it could be sunny one day, snowing the next, and then the rain could come and wash it all away…"

"Yeah, and then it will ice over and cars will crash and people will break their necks…"

"You can be a real grump, you know?" Stella said, wading into the water and submerging herself to wash away the last grains of sand. I followed suit and then we both began our climb back up the rocky hill to collect our bags and make our way home. We'd just reached the outskirts of the forest when a bell chimed.

"Quick, that bell means we've only got two minutes until the rain comes." Stella ran off ahead as I looked up to see a colossal mass of heavy black clouds advancing in our direction. I turned and fled, catching up with Stella just as she reached our street. At that exact moment, the clouds burst open and a torrent of rain fell from the sky. It was as if a bucket had been tipped over our heads. We both screamed and ran towards the door, erupting into the house as a sopping bundle, only to bump straight into the last person I expected to see.

Noah stood still in the hallway, his bronzed, athletic arms crossed. What could he possibly have been doing here? I stood there, paralysed. There was just a glint of amusement in his chocolate brown eyes as he eyed us both silently. Our flimsy summer dresses clung to our soaked bodies and the only sound was the steady patter of water dripping onto the floor. I could feel my cheeks burning and felt a compulsion to flee, but Noah was blocking our escape route and I really didn't want to go back outside and face the storm. I was trapped.

After what seemed like an eternity, Noah eventually spoke. "Lose track of time again did we, sister?" The corners of his mouth turned up into a hint of a smile. "You know, it rains at the same time every day. That may come as a surprise to you…"

Stella gave Noah a withering stare and then turned to me. "Mia, this is my brother, Noah. Noah, this is my friend, Mia."

"I know who she is; we're in the same class, remember?"

Stella pulled a face. "Are you going to get out of our way so we can dry off?"

Noah moved his back against the wall to allow us through. Stella stormed ahead while I tiptoed past, embarrassed. I glanced up at Noah and met his gaze. Our eyes locked, and it felt at that moment like he was trying to read my soul.

I quickly averted my gaze and then the moment was gone, almost as if it had never existed. With my cheeks burning, I fled after Stella and tumbled into her bedroom. She picked a couple of towels up off the floor and threw one in my direction.

"I really don't understand how we're related. He's just so weird. It's like he's from another planet. Oh, no offence," she said, towelling herself dry.

I laughed. "No offence taken."

Stella got changed into dry clothes while I wandered over to the window. Her bedroom was in one of the 'centipede's' legs. The left wall was windowless and faced floor to ceiling, wall to wall glass that overlooked her own private garden. I didn't venture outside as the rain was still coming down in torrents but I could see from where I stood that the grass looked greener already, if that was even possible. The garden faced a vast wall of solar panelling that glistened in the rain.

"Do *you* have any brothers or sisters?" Stella asked, coming to stand next to me at the window.

I shook my head. "No, my parents divorced when I was really young, and neither remarried."

"You're so lucky…"

I looked at her disbelievingly. "I don't think anyone's ever said that to me before."

She sighed. "Noah's my twin, so it feels like I've had to share my entire life with someone else."

"Isn't that nice though, to have someone to share your life with?"

"Maybe if that someone wasn't a total freak…"

"I thought Usonians were meant to be nice all the time."

"We're still human after all. And he is my brother…"

I smiled. "I should get home. The rain seems to be easing and I could really do with a long soak in the tub and some dry clothes."

"Perfect timing. The rain will be over in about fifteen seconds," Stella said looking at her watch. She walked me to the door and kissed me on both cheeks.

"Thank you for taking me out today, it was just what I needed," I said, genuinely grateful.

"You're welcome! Any time…" She smiled widely and waved goodbye as I stepped into the cool, fresh air. I inhaled deeply, almost convinced I could actually feel pure oxygen rush around my blood stream, hitting my head like brain freeze.

I walked the short journey home feeling amazing. Despite the long hike and the swim, I seemed to have more energy. Maybe there was something in this healthy eating and exercise business after all.

After a long bath and a fresh change of clothes, I wandered into the kitchen to make dinner. We hadn't needed lunch after the huge breakfast, but the active day had made me ravenous. I ate a mammoth dinner and then collapsed on the sofa to read until GG came home. Once he'd eaten, we settled in to play board games and ended up staying awake until the early hours.

The rest of the weekend was relaxed and easy. I had a sublime sleep-in on Sunday and then read the newspaper over a breakfast of orange juice and a feta, spinach and mushroom omelette. I helped GG in the garden for the afternoon, tending the vegetables and picking some out for dinner later. I thought about how I spent my weekends on Earth and there was a stark contrast. I'd usually be out with my friends, holed up in a shopping centre, or sat drinking sugary drinks and eating greasy burgers at one of the countless fast food restaurants. If I was at home I'd either be attached to my computer, phone or the TV, sat in a dark room, unmoving from the sofa. It seemed a lifetime ago now. At the end of my five day weekend, I stood in front of the mirror and could see I was starting to look different. The whites of my eyes looked brighter and the dark circles underneath had disappeared. There was a subtle glow to my skin and my cheeks had a hint of rosiness to them. I took a hot shower and climbed into bed early so that I was fresh for school the next day and fell quickly into a heavy, contented sleep.

Chapter 9

"Good morning, class!" Mr Kepler called cheerily. "I trust all of your weekends were nice and relaxing."

The class was humming with the excited exchange of teenagers who hadn't seen each other for half the week. The noise quietened down as Mr Kepler spoke again.

"Today's first lesson is going to be all about politics!" My heart sank and I looked around the classroom expecting these words to be met with rolling eyes and groans of disappointment. But everyone was leaning forward in their seats in excited anticipation. Maybe politics meant something different on Usonia. No school child on Earth would ever have had this reaction. I glanced in the direction of Noah, being painstakingly careful not to catch his eye, but he was resolutely facing forward, expressionless as ever.

"Now, Mia, this will be a very useful lesson for you. You see, Usonia is run a little differently to Earth, and I think it will be helpful for you to have some context... So, without further ado, let's get into the history of politics and economics of our planet!

"Politics on Usonia is, understandably, constantly evolving. Our founding fathers arrived to an uninhabited planet where, of course, no political or economic systems were in place. As you well know, Project Ark was an initiative funded by numerous governments, and the first settlers had no means to trade or earn their own income. Because of this, the first inhabitants began life on the planet as communists. Would anyone like to define communism for me?"

This time I was unsurprised to see all hands shoot up. Only Noah and myself refrained, and of course Mr Kepler targeted Noah first. I was beginning to see a pattern.

"Mr Maxwell?" he said, looking expectantly at Noah.

Noah was silent for a moment, nothing about his demeanour giving away what he was thinking, and then he spoke clearly and unwaveringly. "Communism is a political system where everything is shared amongst the community – from workload, through to produce and property. People carry out the work they're best suited to, and then goods are divided among the people as needed."

"Thank you, Noah. A very nice explanation. In simple terms, the first Usonians received a wage from

Earth. They worked together to build a sustainable community, producing to meet demand, and sharing the workload and the wealth accordingly.

"As time wore on, Earth's governments relinquished their control over Usonia, and with that came a reduction in funding. The Bank of Usonia was established in 1970 and the national currency became the means by which inhabitants could trade for goods and services. Free trade and competition were encouraged as a means to improve productivity and quality, however capitalist hierarchies were avoided by the introduction of linear organisational structures, vertical business models and common ownership. Can anyone explain the difference between the linear and vertical business models?"

A raven haired boy at the front of the class was picked out of the sea of hands, and he stood up to answer. "A linear business structure is when no job is seen as more or less important than another. Everyone is equal in the business."

"That's right, Al," Mr Kepler said. "With a linear structure, all roles within the business are considered equal and necessary to its success. No middle or senior management exist, which wipes out inefficiency and duplication, and all profits are shared equally between the workers. Now, who can tell me about vertical structures? Go ahead, Stella."

Stella looked delighted to have been picked. She took a deep breath and enthusiastically launched into her explanation. "A vertical business structure is where everyone within the business is involved from start to finish, so for example in farming, all workers help prepare the land, sow the seeds, water and tend to the crops, harvest them, and then take the goods or produce to market and sell them. The seller can keep what they earn or all takings can be shared."

"Very good, Miss Maxwell. So you see, economically, Usonia has evolved to become a more socialist society, while still embracing the competition and free trade that capitalism brings." Mr Kepler looked at me then. "Is this making sense to you, Mia?"

All eyes turned towards me and I blushed furiously. "Yes, Mr Kepler, perfect sense." I could feel Noah's eyes burning into me but I refused to meet his gaze. I kept my eyes firmly on the visuals of workers that danced across my screen, until Mr Kepler began to speak again.

"As the population grew, the running of the planet itself became more and more difficult to manage, without a structure in place. Usonia was, and will always be, governed by its people, and so forming a traditional government with some sort of overarching ruler was not an option. It was eventually decided that an administering body would be formed. We called this body simply, The Administration. Every single inhabitant of Usonia is, at least once in their lifetime, invited to join The Administration. Similar to jury duty on Earth, but rather than make it compulsory, it has always been seen as a right and a privilege. No Usonian so far has turned down the invitation.

"I expect you're wondering, without a government and ruler, how do decisions get made? Well, this is where it gets interesting."

I highly doubted that, but his enthusiasm was infectious, so I was still just about managing to pay attention.

"In most societies on Earth, members of the population are invited to elect a representative to make political decisions on their behalf. They are known as MPs or Members of Parliament, and, once elected, they attend Parliament to vote for and against various proposals, or even present their own proposals. Disappointingly, those people in Parliament only represent a very small, and mostly privileged section of society. The bulk of the population is under-represented in Parliament, and this is bad news when this is the place where huge, world-changing decisions are made.

"Making decisions in this way made at least some sense in the past, but since the technological revolution, it really is just as easy to ask every member of the population for their opinion, rendering MPs and Parliament effectively obsolete. On Usonia, every single individual aged eleven plus is given the opportunity to vote on major issues in an online referendum. No major decision is passed without going to referendum, turning Usonia into more of a direct democracy. Many smaller issues or items that need to be attended to quickly are made public on the bulletin board and Usonians are usually given ten days to object. If more than ten percent of the population objects, a referendum will be called. Otherwise, the administrators will simply implement the proposal. It's very simple but we've found it makes the running of our planet mostly harmonious. Wouldn't you agree, class?"

Everyone started murmuring and nodding. It made perfect sense to me. I couldn't understand why you needed to be over eighteen to vote in elections. If we were old enough to work, get married, have children and drive a car, all before the age of eighteen, then we were old enough to vote on issues that had a direct impact on us. Although I could remember my granddad telling me that even if the person you voted for got into power, there was nothing holding them to their election promises anyway.

I thought the political system on Usonia was inspired. I couldn't believe I was going to get to vote on something that affected the whole planet, instead of being treated like a stupid child with no opinion and no rights. Everything I learned about this planet made me question what people were doing down on Earth and made me thankful that I was here living on this planet.

Mr Kepler broke my reverie. "The next referendum will take place on Monday, and this will be a very big day for our newest resident, Miss McAdams." He looked at me and smiled encouragingly. "In the meantime, class, I want you to get into pairs and spend the next hour developing your own enterprise idea. I'd like to see how your businesses would be structured as both linear and vertical models, and then you can present them to the rest of the class."

My second week of school sailed by even more quickly than the first. I'd finally stopped feeling constantly exhausted. Maybe the interplanetary jetlag had passed, or maybe there was just something in the air and the water here. I almost felt like I was rejuvenating with each day. My mind was becoming sharper, my memory better. I was quickly absorbing the new languages and had stopped dreading going to school, instead I looked forward to it.

I learned that the raven haired boy in my class was named Alpha, although everyone called him Al for short. I'd been paired with him for our group activity and he was as friendly and warm as all the other Usonians. Except, of course, for Noah, who wasn't actually unfriendly as such, just somewhat detached. I hadn't quite figured him out yet. I had to keep reminding myself that he was Stella's brother; they were complete opposites.

I was indirectly the talk of the school that week. GG was holding his 95th birthday party at our house on Saturday and it was all anyone could talk about. I felt incredibly popular, if only by association. Stella invited herself over after school on Friday to design our outfits for the party. She arrived with a humongous bag, teeming with assorted fabrics, and a sewing machine in tow.

She flung everything out onto the bed and began sorting through undyed material. "I was picturing you in silk. Layers and layers of it! I picked some fruit from my garden and I was thinking we could crush them up and colour your dress berry red. What do you say?"

I opened my mouth to answer but it quickly became clear that it was a rhetorical question. Before I could speak, she'd already begun wrapping me with her tape measure and draping silk over my shoulders. Stella pulled me around like a rag doll for a while and then stood back to admire her work, looking satisfied. Her mouth full of pins, she silently and determinedly unpinned the fabric from me. She ushered me off to prepare the dye, shouting instructions as I was leaving the room, and then sat down at the sewing machine.

In the kitchen, I mashed the berries in a pan of water as it began to boil. After letting it simmer for a little while, I strained the liquid to remove all the skin and seeds and then carefully poured it into a large bowl. I carried it into the utility room to find Stella already waiting, holding my dress folded in her hands. She plunged it into the hot dye and then shoed me away. "No peaking! I want it to be a surprise."

I went back into my room and had just finished clearing up the mess Stella had made when she reappeared, swooning. "It's going to look amazing! I've hung it outside to dry. Let's go and make a matching lip colour while we're waiting." She grabbed a smaller paper bag full of berries and then pulled me into the kitchen. We spent the rest of the evening blending beeswax, almond butter, olive oil and berries to make a lipstick that perfectly matched my dress. We worked late into the night before Stella started yawning and checked her watch.

"Wow, is that the time? We should get our beauty sleep for the party tomorrow. I'll take your dress home with me and come over early tomorrow to help you get ready." She kissed me on the cheek and then vanished before I had a chance to object.

The next morning, GG allowed me to sleep in a little before waking me up to go to the market.

"Rise and shine, dear! We've got lots of shopping to do before the party tonight," he said, poking his head around the door.

I looked at him blurry eyed. I'd been waking up naturally from the sun ever since I arrived on Usonia, but it was much higher in the sky than usual so I must have over-slept.

I rubbed my eyes and then slid out of bed, following him into the kitchen. I swiped my arm in front of the cooker and it swiftly dished me up a breakfast full of berries and oats and coconut yoghurt. I took it to the table and sat opposite GG, using all of my strength to lift my head.

GG shook his head smiling. "Did you girls have a late night?"

I nodded sleepily. "We were making clothes for the party. It was Stella's idea."

"Maybe you can have a nap this afternoon. You'll need to be fresh for the party; everyone will want to meet you, young lady. I won't disturb you - I need to spend a few hours finishing off my rebuttal against Conan's proposal this afternoon, anyway."

"Conan?"

"Remember I told you last week about that dastardly government official that's making my life hell? The one intent on damaging Usonia by speeding up construction so that they can begin the migration from Earth sooner?"

"I remember... Is he really called Conan?" It didn't seem a very Earthling-like name.

"Of course not; that's just what we call him. The Barbarian. The Destroyer. You see?"

I stared back blankly.

"Well, anyway, the next meeting is on Wednesday via satellite. I need to put a damn good case together to prevent this ignorant, impatient man from undoing all of our hard work. His proposal would have disastrous consequences for the entire human race."

I looked at GG and felt completely helpless. He looked so downhearted. He met my concerned gaze for a moment and then snapped himself out of it, smiling cheerily. "No point getting all upset about it, I suppose; that never solved anything..." He stood up. "Now! We've got a party to prepare for. Go and get yourself dressed, we'll head off to the markets as soon as you're ready."

We went to the markets on foot, each pulling a fabric trolley full of empty glass containers in varying sizes.

"What's all this for?" I asked, nodding at the trolley I was lugging behind me.

"We don't like waste on Usonia, so nothing is sold packaged. Rather than the mass recycling that exists on Earth, we limit production and consumption instead, so waste barely exists."

We arrived at the market square to be greeted by rows and rows of canvas and timber market stalls, overflowing with fresh produce, cheeses and opulent woven fabrics. There were buckets of fresh coconut yoghurt sat in crates of ice, vast pitchers of milk and juices ready to be bottled, tubs of gooey honey, and heavy looking sacks full of various grains. Fragrance and makeup were laid out in ornate glass decanters and bowls, available to purchase by the gram. On the opposite side were stalls full of raw materials. Untreated wood, balls of clay, tubs of sand, and metals glinting in the sunshine. It was the most magical market I'd ever experienced.

We filled our sacks and containers with everything we needed for the party and for the coming week, throwing huge, bright and lush-looking fruit and vegetables into our bags.

"Why do the fruit and vegetables look so strange here?" I asked GG, twisting a crooked red pepper around in my hand.

GG laughed. "It's because they're grown naturally and organically on Usonia. On Earth, so much of the produce is genetically modified or full of chemicals, so that it looks aesthetically perfect, but tastes like, well, like nothing really. Fruit and vegetables on Usonia might look unsightly, but they're full of flavour, and they're better for your health too." He threw some apples and pears into his trolley. "Of course, we're very lucky here. We have optimum conditions for farming... The right levels of sunlight and wind, a perfectly balanced eco system, and we can control the rain to prevent drought and flooding. There's absolutely no reason to mess with farming using chemicals. Unless of course, Conan gets his way, and we suddenly need to start producing enough food to feed the masses," GG added, with a note of anguish in his voice. We continued shopping silently after that, GG deep in thought, mentally preparing for his meeting with Conan.

After a lunch of beetroot, walnut, feta and spinach salad, I left GG to his work and went for nap before the party. I'd only intended to sleep for an hour but awoke when it was almost getting dark. I leapt out of bed and quickly ran myself a bubble bath. I was just wrapping myself in a thick cotton towel when Stella arrived.

"Perfect timing! Let's get started." She sat me down in front of the dresser and pulled out a box full of her own home-made makeup. She spent the next thirty minutes working some kind of miracle on my pale and uninteresting face and then coaxed and teased my hair into voluminous waves. She let me get changed coyly in my dressing room, shaking her head at my neuroses, and then applied the finishing touches with a splash of berry red lip colour.

She led me towards the full length mirror and then spun me around. The transformation was quite literally astonishing. A stranger stared back at me from the mirror, eyes wide in amazement. Stella had painted my eye lids with smoky makeup that made my small grey eyes look huge and Bambi-like. My normally flat hair looked full, shiny and glamorous. The berry lips somehow made my hair appear dark and sultry, instead of the mousy nothingness I usually saw. The dress was incredible. It was fitted and strapless, kicking out at my hips into layers and folds of jagged raw silk. My face broke into a wide smile; I felt like a princess. For the first time since arriving on Usonia, I thought I might actually look like I belonged here. No longer the eternal outsider.

That desperate hope lasted until about three minutes into the party. I found myself being passed around from guest to guest, forced to smile sweetly while answering mind-numbing questions about life on Earth. There was no escaping it, I was definitely from another planet.

I was just looking around desperately for an escape route, when the front door opened, and I found myself staring straight at none other than Noah Maxwell.

Chapter 10

I swung back around and dived faux-enthusiastically into conversation with my neighbours. I didn't know why it hadn't occurred to me that Noah would be at this party. Everyone else in the city seemed to be here. It just hadn't even crossed my mind that he would be here - in *my* house. It took some time for my heartbeat to slow to normal and for my mind to clear, before I could begin to think straight. I didn't really understand the effect this boy was having on me, it was something new and strange and totally indescribable.

I'd almost fully recovered when Stella grabbed my arm and excitedly pulled me over to meet her parents. A grand-looking woman with a sharp flame-coloured bob and an elegant linen suit kissed me warmly on both cheeks. "You must be Mia. I've heard such a lot about you, darling; Stella talks about you non-stop. My name's Cassiopeia, but please call me Peia. And this is my husband, Neo." She pulled Neo out from the corner and he clapped both of his hands around my small fingers. I tried not to wince, and formed my features into a winning smile, painfully aware that Noah had just joined his family and was looking at me with a hint of amusement in his eyes.

"Welcome to our planet, my dear, I do hope you're settling in nicely. Have you met our boy, Noah?" I opened my mouth to speak but no words came out.

"We're in the same class at school, Pa…. Hi Mia." Noah gave me a shy smile and leaned in to greet me with a kiss. I think I might actually have stopped breathing for a moment.

I was saved by the sound of ringing glass slicing through the hum, before Priscilla began to speak, practically bubbling over with enthusiasm. "On behalf of the great Herbert McAdams, I'd like to welcome you all, and thank you for joining us in celebrating this very special day. Today, we celebrate Herb's 95th birthday, and also commemorate his 65th year on the beautiful planet we call home."

I'd been steered around so that we could have a better view of Priscilla and the speeches, but in the process, I'd somehow ended up side by side with Noah. His bronzed arm was resting about a millimetre from mine and it made the hairs on my arm stand on end. I could hear his slow rhythmic breathing and could smell a hint of deep musk. It was dizzying.

Priscilla went on, "Herb has achieved so much in his lifetime that it's difficult to know where to begin. So much of what he has accomplished is simply part of our daily life and it's easy to take it all for granted. We have Herb to thank for our incredible underground transport system. He worked with engineers throughout the 1950s to develop a system that is 100% sustainable and has resulted in zero accidents since operation began. The concept has left the beautiful surface of our planet safe and free for people and animals to roam freely."

The crowd surged forward so that they could hear Priscilla more clearly and my arm bumped Noah's for a split second. It was like an electric shock shot through me and I stepped to the side, putting a safe distance between us. I glanced at Noah out of the corner of my eye. He was looking straight ahead, his eyes twinkling and a smile playing at the corners of his mouth.

"Herb worked with architects from the very first days he arrived on this planet to ensure every home and work place is self-sufficient and capable of meeting its own energy needs. That incredible fresh air that fills your lungs with every breath is all down to Herb here. He has increased human life expectancy on this planet by over twenty five percent, with not a single person dying before they reached their 90s. I'm sure you'll all agree, he's improved our standards of living ten fold. He has worked tirelessly for the past 65 years to create a harmonious community where it seems that we want for nothing. And he still continues to fight to protect us and the planet we call home today. Never losing faith, and always with a smile on his face. Herb, you have been an inspiration to all of us, and Usonia would not be the planet it was today, if it weren't for you." Priscilla raised her glass, "Please join me now in a toast to our own Herbert McAdams... To Herb!"

Everyone around us raised their glasses and yelled out, "To Herb!"

GG joined Priscilla and the cheers and applause died down. He cleared his throat. "I cannot even begin to describe how happy I am that so many of you are here to join us in celebrating today. As you know, this year commemorates the 65th year since we, the founding fathers, landed on Usonia. We arrived on a foreign planet, with no idea what to expect, and the weight of a huge task ahead of us. We all left countless loved ones behind and slowly began to build new families and communities along the way. It was never easy, but we were all here with a common goal, and so we pulled together and never gave up hope. It brings a tear to my eye today to stand here before you all, remembering all of those great pioneers who gave up everything to help make Usonia the idyllic planet that we have the privilege of inhabiting today... I'd like to raise a toast." My great grandfather paused for a moment, swallowing the emotion, and then raised his glass. "In memory of those of us who cannot be with us today... To the late founding fathers of Usonia."

I practically choked the words as the crowd murmured, "To the late founding fathers."

"And now, I think a celebration is in order! Eat, drink, dance and be merry. A fellow only turns 95 once in a life time!" GG beamed widely and the atmosphere visibly lifted. A band struck up and delicious-looking canapés began circulating the room on trays. Glasses were topped up with colourful cocktails made from fresh juices, herbs and spices, and the guests began to mingle again.

Mrs Maxwell turned to me and pulled Noah by his elbow to join us. "Mia, it's just occurred to me, I wonder, have you had the chance to visit the district of Nata yet?"

"Um, I don't think so… I've only been here for a couple of weeks, there hasn't really been the time for much sight seeing."

She touched Noah's arm. "Darling, you must take Mia there." She turned back to me. "It's Noah's absolute favourite place in the world." Noah gave her what could only be described as some sort of death stare. "Some company would be good for you, darling. You spend too much time alone, and I'm sure Mia could use some friends. Think of the poor girl. She's left her parents behind, all of her friends…"

Noah's expression softened and he looked at me with new eyes. "Only if Mia wants to…"

"She'd love to! Wouldn't you Mia? How about next Saturday? Come over to our place at around 11am and you can take our cap. There, it's decided! You'll just love it."

I opened and closed my mouth like a goldfish and then eventually managed to get out the words, "That sounds… nice, thank you…"

A waiter walked by with a tray of canapés and I grabbed one and threw it in my mouth to avoid Noah's gaze. Stella grabbed my hand. "Let's go and dance; I love this song!" And I was relieved to be led away.

"My mum is such a pest sometimes, I'm sorry... It's just Noah is so socially awkward, I think she was hoping you might be good for him. She's desperate for him to make some friends and live a normal life... Oh look, there's Al!" She waved for him to join us on the dance floor and he bounded over eagerly, dropping his empty plate onto the nearest table.

The three of us danced like crazy people for what felt like hours. Stella and I took it in turns to be twirled and swung around by Al, shaking our hair and spinning around in circles. I hadn't had so much fun in a really long time. Every now and then I'd catch sight of Noah, his back against the wall, looking ostensibly disinterested, but every time Al touched my hand, I could feel his eyes burning into me. We danced and ate and drank into the early hours, and when the final guests went home, I collapsed on my bed, giddy from the combination of potent fruit juices, music and dancing.

The next few days mostly consisted of recovery and operation clean up. Priscilla and Stella dropped by to help and together we pulled down reams of bunting and boxed it all up ready for reuse. We collected candles and took them to the workshop to be melted down and reset. Food scraps were taken out for composting, and the dishwasher was constantly loaded and reloaded with plates and glasses.

By the time Monday flew around, it seemed as though the weekend had disappeared in a blink. I felt a flash of disappointment that the weekend was over, but it was quickly replaced with anticipation as I remembered that it was voting day.

At school, the atmosphere was different to usual. There was a quiet buzz of expectation instead of the usual excitement and enthusiasm. Almost an air of solemnity amongst the students. Stella was unusually early and the entire class was already seated by the time I entered the room. All eyes turned to me as I closed the door behind me. I looked at Mr Kepler apologetically but he waved me in, smiling.

"Don't worry, Mia, you're not late. The students are just usually extra keen on voting days. If you're a minute late, you don't get to vote and essentially lose your voice. There's still plenty of time. Get yourself settled in and ready to have your say in the way Usonia is run."

I made my way to my seat. Al beamed in my direction and Stella waved at me enthusiastically. I snuck a peak at Noah and he smiled at me, mouthing the word, "Hi."

I mouthed, "Hey," back and a smile reflexively crept up around my mouth. It was a relief that he was speaking to me, since his mother had pushed us both into hanging out together on Saturday. It would be just awful if we spent the day in awkward silence.

"Ok, class, countdown to the live broadcast starts soon," Mr Kepler said, clapping his hands together. "Mia, the topic of the vote is always kept confidential until the public broadcast. This is so that opinions can't be swayed and your vote will be true, honest and your own. The presentation you're about to watch will be broadcasted live to all schools, workplaces and public buildings in Usonia. It will be made by an independent adjudicator who'll state the facts and then list the pros and cons for everyone and everything that this proposal could affect, both now and in the future. So make sure you listen carefully! Class, there will be no speaking until you have placed your votes, in ten, nine, eight..."

Everyone began to shuffle in their seats, clearing their throats and hushing each other. Once the count reached zero, all screens came alive with a visual of a severe-looking woman dressed in a deep brown suit. She had a shock of cropped white hair and latte coloured skin, with a strong, athletic build. The room was so silent you could hear the wind rustling the trees outside.

"Good morning, fellow Usonians," the lady on the screen said, crisply and clearly, almost as if she were automated. "My name is Astrid Wright and I will be your independent adjudicator throughout today's referendum. Thank you to every one of you who has assembled at institutions across the planet today. Your unblinking allegiance to Usonia never goes unrecognised. Thank you for your patience. Today's referendum topic is as follows... The Administration is proposing to design and build an open air amphitheatre on the western outskirts of Paramount City. The purpose of this is to inspire creativity in citizens as well as provide entertainment to residents. Usonians wishing to book the space for a performance would freely be able to do so via The Administration's electronic booking system. They may then either provide free entertainment or can charge residents for the entertainment as they see fit."

The possible negatives were listed first. They included an additional tax of 1% for the next six months and surface damage to the face of the planet. The positives included job creation for the construction and management of the amphitheatre, a boost to the economy with potential income from performances, a creative outlet for Usonians, and entertainment for the masses – critical as Usonia grows.

The screens on our desks flicked to an overview of the proposal in three columns – one for the facts, one for the pros and lastly the cons. Underneath sat five voting buttons.

The adjudicator spoke again, "Now that you have heard the facts, you have several options. If you are for the proposal, simply press 'Yes' on your touch screen. Likewise, if you are completely against the idea, please just touch the icon labelled 'No'. If you are neither for nor against the proposal, you have three options. If you have no opinion on the matter and it does not concern you if the proposal is or isn't passed, you are permitted to select the 'Divided' icon. If you feel that there are more questions that need to be answered, you can press the 'Questions' button and then enter your questions for consideration. Lastly, if you feel that there is another alternative that could reach the same outcome, please choose the 'Alternative' icon and then make your suggestion. If the vote produces a straight decision, we will be able to communicate that to you as soon as voting is complete. If the referendum throws up more questions or alternatives, The Administration will revisit the proposal and a second referendum will be held. You now have a maximum of five minutes to read over the information summarised on your screens and place your votes."

Chapter 11

I agonised over my vote, desperately wanting to get it right. I felt the weight of responsibility hanging like a heavy rain cloud over my head. A part of me thought it would be nice to have some kind of entertainment space, something new for people to do here on the planet. But I didn't pay taxes and I felt bad imposing an extra financial burden on everyone else. I didn't want to place a neutral vote and I couldn't think of any questions that needed to be answered... but maybe there was an alternative solution. There could be a natural bowl shape that exists somewhere on the planet that we could use as an amphitheatre. It would cost less to build and less harm would come to the planet and the eco system. The adjudicator announced that we had 60 seconds remaining so I quickly decided to press the 'Alternative' icon. The screen prompted me to type in my recommendation and I quickly tapped out my idea.

The adjudicator counted down from ten to the close of voting. As she reached zero, our screens automatically switched off. On the main screen, the adjudicator spoke.

"Thank you for voting, fellow Usonians. All votes are now in, and in just a few moments, I will have the results for you." She paused, waiting for the automatic count to appear, and then our screens lit up with a bar chart displaying the results. "It looks like we're back to the drawing board, neighbours. Alternative site options will now be sought elsewhere on the planet. The shortlist will be presented to you for voting in the coming weeks. Thank you and have a good day."

The screen flashed and then turned to black. A buzz of conversation struck up around the room and I felt a vague thrill that my suggestion was being taken on board. It was so rare to feel like I was part of something important and that my opinion actually counted.

Saturday morning arrived all too quickly. One half of me was really looking forward to spending the day with Noah. The other half was nothing short of terrified. Every time I thought about it, nervous energy bubbled and fluttered up into my chest.

Out of habit, I looked out of the window to check the weather, but it was another perfect day. I pulled on a khaki cotton jumpsuit and some white tennis shoes and then inspected myself in the mirror. I pulled my hair back into a bun and then promptly shook it out again. I plaited it down one side of my neck, looked at

117

myself critically, and then unplaited it again. I tipped my hair upside down and ruffled it to get some volume, then teased it into place. I dabbed some berry lipstick onto my mouth and stood back. I looked completely ridiculous. I wiped the lipstick off with the back of my hand and then grabbed the brush, scraped my hair back into a pony tail and walked away from the mirror before I could do any more damage. I picked up my canvas bag and then checked the time. My stomach twisted. I was going to be late. I was tempted to crawl back into bed and stay there beneath a protective tent of blankets, but I forced myself out of the door before I could change my mind.

I walked to Noah's house at a decreasingly slow pace. I arrived to find him leaning against his front porch looking devastatingly nonchalant. His eyes danced when he saw me and I felt an involuntary flutter in my middle. He waved his hand once from left to right and then ambled down the steps to meet me. His hand pressed the small of my back as he leaned in to kiss my cheek and I thought my knees were going to buckle. Before I'd had chance to speak or even move, he had walked off towards the garage and was pulling open the door.

"I thought I'd save you from getting trapped by my family by diverting you away from the house," Noah said, swiping his watch at the door of the cap and then standing back for me to climb in first.

"I like your family," I protested as I clambered in, trying to look elegant as he watched, and failing miserably.

"I know you do." He smiled and slid in next to me.

The door snapped shut and a moment later my stomach was in my throat as we zoomed at high speed down into the ground. We bounced lightly as we reached the bottom of the tube, hovering for a few moments as we waited for a clear run, and then the cap thrust forward at the green light.

"It's much more fun taking the loop with you," Noah spoke and I turned to look at him questioningly. He was watching me with a glint of amusement in his eyes. "You're so expressive... It makes you really interesting to watch. You hardly ever speak, but you say so much without having to use any words at all."

"You hardly ever talk either," I retorted, a little accusingly, but he just laughed.

"Does it bother you?"

"No... Not at all." I thought about it for a moment, and I realised that I meant it. "It's actually quite nice. Everyone else on this planet talks non-stop all of the time. It's kind of... peaceful, being with you."

"I'll stop ruining it for you then..."

"I didn't mean that," I said, blushing.

"I'm just teasing you. You're an easy target."

The cap slowed to a stop and Noah stood up. "I'm taking you the scenic route to Nata by the way; hope your shoes are good for walking." He looked me up and down, assessing my outfit, and I felt the blood rushing to my cheeks again. The door swung open and he gestured towards it. "After you…"

"No, *please*, after you." I sat resolutely still until he gave in and climbed out first, shaking his head.

Noah was so unexpectedly cheerful and chatty that it threw me off guard at the start, but I soon relaxed and began to feel at ease in his company. It felt good to be myself for a change. I hadn't realised it until now, but the entire time I'd been on Usonia, I'd been putting up some kind of front. A façade. I was so desperate for people to like me that I'd hardly dared to let my true self show.

Noah walked quickly ahead, turning back occasionally to check that I was still following. I had to jog to keep up every now and then, he was much faster than Stella. I hadn't noticed it happen but I could easily walk at Stella's pace without breaking into a sweat now.

We strode forward in the direction of a valley running between two rocky hills. As we approached, the wind picked up and I was glad I'd tied my hair back and worn a pant suit. My pony tail was swinging around like a propeller. Once we'd passed through the valley, Noah turned back and smiled. "Turn around."

As I spun around, twin verdant mountainous peaks loomed into view, towering over us. Gradually, I became aware of a low distant hum mixed in with the whistle of the wind and I looked closely at the hills. Suddenly, rows and rows of vertical wind turbines came into view, like I was staring at a magic eye picture.

"Do you see them?" Noah asked, watching my expression intently.

My eyes lit up and I turned to him. "This is truly amazing."

His eyes danced back at me. "Beautiful aren't they? These wind turbines are made from glass so they blend in with the landscape better. You have to look really closely, but once you see them, they're mesmerising. All spinning around, off beat and out of step with each other, but still all connected, working together to create energy and power... It's one of my favourite places to come and think."

We stood silent and still, watching the turbines work together. They coiled upwards as corkscrews, spinning softly and elegantly like ballerinas. I was hypnotised. I could hear Noah breathing softly next to me, feel his body heat radiating, and I felt truly calm for the first time I could ever remember.

Noah turned away from the mountains, beckoning for me to follow him, and I reluctantly tore myself away. "Come on, I'm saving the best 'til last."

We ploughed on and gradually something strange appeared in the distance. It looked like a giant white fluffy blanket spread out across the ground. I glanced at Noah but he just looked straight ahead, his eyes twinkling. As we got closer, the blanket seemed to almost pixelate and it started to look like it was made up of millions of small white flowers. As we reached the field, I realised they weren't flowers at all. What lay in front of me was a sea of brown twigs decorated with balls of cotton wool.

Noah turned to me. "Have you ever seen cotton fields before?"

I looked at him, stunned. "This is cotton?"

He laughed loudly. "*This* is cotton." He snapped off a stalk that held three little balls of cotton and handed it to me like a bunch of flowers. I grinned stupidly. It was the ugliest bouquet I'd ever seen but it made my middle flutter.

Noah looked at his watch and then up at the sky. I followed his gaze to see an army of black clouds rolling over the hills, charging in our direction.

"We'd better get out of here, quick." He grabbed my hand and before I had time to think, I was pulled off in the direction of a timber building in the middle of the field. We reached the hut at lightening speed and Noah twisted the handle, slamming his body into the door. We practically fell into the room just as water began crashing down from the skies. We stood still for a moment, catching our breath, before simultaneously realising that my hand was still in Noah's. We both let go as if we'd just noticed we were holding hot rocks, and I pushed my way into the room so he couldn't see the colour in my cheeks.

Noah made himself busy in the kitchen and began pulling things out of the cupboard. "Hungry?" he asked, turning to me.

"Starving, actually."

"I'm not surprised, we've probably walked around eight kilometres already today."

I sat at the table while Noah piled bread, cheese and grapes onto a plate. He placed it between us and then brought over two glasses of water and sat down.

"Should we be in here?" I asked, suddenly feeling like I was trespassing.

"Usonians aren't as possessive as Earthlings. We like to share and help each other. I think it stems from the founding fathers where everyone had to share everything, so it became inherent in their children. This hut is for the workers in the fields, but they don't work weekends so it's left empty. They leave it unlocked and keep the cupboards well stocked for visitors."

"It really is a different world," I said, spreading cheese onto some bread and devouring it hungrily.

"Tell me about your life on Earth, were you happy there?"

"I loved it there, truly. I have a best friend called Ellie, but she's more like a sister really. We both cried when I had to leave. She's silly and scatter-brained and loud, kind of the opposite to me, which is why I think we make such good friends." I pushed a grape into my mouth and swallowed before continuing. "I loved my school. I wasn't top of the class or anything, but I liked learning new things, and I had a lot of friends. Everyone on Earth complains about the weather madly, but I actually kind of miss it."

"It does get kind of boring here, doesn't it? You always know it's going to be a sunny day and you know exactly when it's going to rain. Some unpredictability would be more interesting, I think."

"Exactly. I never thought I'd say this, but I miss wrapping up warm in a scarf and gloves, feeling the icy breeze on my cheeks, seeing my breath in the air…" I fell silent at the memory of my home planet, leaving just the sound of the rain lashing down all around us.

"Do you miss your family? I know you have your great grandfather here, but it must be hard without your mum and dad." Noah spoke softly and waited for me to gather my thoughts.

"It's strange. I never met my great grandfather before arriving on Usonia, but it's like we've known each other my whole life. He really feels like family; I'm so lucky to have him. But I do miss my parents… I didn't get to see my dad very often so it hasn't really hit home that I might never see him again. I'm weirdly used to missing him, so that's kind of normal. But my mum… I was so, so angry at her for sending me here, for letting me go, that it's almost made it easier for me. I saw her every day of my life. Even if it was just doing mundane things, we were still together every day. Hating her is far less painful than the alternative." I didn't want to have to think about my family anymore so I switched the subject over to Noah. "Tell me about your family."

Noah gave me a small smile and sighed softly. "I love my family, of course I do… But I often find myself wondering if we're really related. Sometimes I think my parents must have found me on another

124

planet." He laughed sombrely. "It's hard being a twin too, especially when that twin is so outgoing and loud and, well, popular. The polar opposite to me. It's almost like she saps the energy out of me. The more confident she is, the more I seem to retreat into myself. It's easier to just step back and let her take centre stage. I'm kind of a loner really. I usually prefer it that way."

"That was the first thing I noticed about you. That you're different to everyone else."

"Like you." He looked at me with those eyes. The ones that seemed to be able to read me like no-one else could.

"But I try so hard to fit in. I really want to belong here."

"And I'd rather be anywhere else." He gazed at me searchingly. "I like talking to you, Mia. I feel like I can be honest with you. You don't judge."

The noise of the rain began to ease and seconds later, the hut was in complete silence, almost as if the rain had been turned off like a tap. Noah pushed back his chair and began collecting the plates, putting them into the dishwasher while I wiped down the table.

"Ready to experience the district of Nata?" Noah asked with a grin and then pulled open the door without waiting for me to answer. He marched off ahead but then looked back and noticed me struggling to keep up. He slowed down to match my pace. "Tell me about your childhood, Mia. What's your first memory?"

"My first memory... Hmmm, that's a difficult one. I have flashes of memories from when I was around three years old, but I think I must have been about six by the time I had my first clear memory. I can remember my mum had sent Dad out to buy some milk so she could make the cheese sauce for our dinner. He took me with him, scooping me up and throwing me over his shoulder. I can remember squealing in delight while my mother scolded Dad, telling him to be careful. As we approached the shops, I remember seeing a poster tied to a lamp post. On it was a picture of a puppy sitting beneath the words 'Lost' scrawled in a child's hand writing. The poster was begging for anyone who had seen him to get in touch. I pulled at my dad's coat and asked if we could go and look for the puppy.

"He said, 'No darling, we'll get in trouble with Mum. We'd better get the milk and hurry home for dinner.' But I begged and pleaded. I could see him relenting, so I carried on and eventually he agreed. We traipsed around the houses and parks for almost an hour and then we spotted him. His lead was tangled around a fence and he was whining and shivering. I remember turning to my dad delighted. We both looked at each other and then ran towards the dog. My dad unravelled his lead and picked him up, tucking him inside his coat to keep him warm. We called the number on the poster, returned the dog to his owners and then plodded back home through the dark, cold night.

"Mum was furious when we got back. The dinner was ruined and I can remember her slamming things around the kitchen before she stormed upstairs. I didn't see her for the rest of the evening. I think that was the beginning of the end of their relationship..." I smiled sadly and then looked at Noah. "What's yours?"

He laughed. "I'm beginning to regret I asked you that question... Stella and I were five years old. It was our school play and we were performing Noah's Ark. Of course, I was Noah."

"Isn't Noah's Ark a religious story? I didn't think you believed in religion on Usonia."

"We don't. We see bible stories as fairy tales, kind of like the Brothers Grimm. So, I was playing the lead in our school play and obviously I hated it. I can't think of anything worse than being the centre of attention, but I was just kind of pushed into it. Stella was playing the back end of a goat and I can remember her being really disappointed, but of course she's too nice to say anything."

I laughed and then straightened my face.

"On the day, I forgot one of my lines. My brain had gone completely blank and I just stood there, frozen. The whole hall sat in silence for what felt like an eternity, and then Stella stepped backwards out of her goat suit and poked her head out. The whole room erupted into laughter. She'd been helping me practise at home and could tell I'd forgotten the words, even though she couldn't see a thing. She mouthed the words to me and then it all came flooding back. She climbed back into her suit, I said my line and the rest of the play went off without a hitch. And, of course, Stella had become the real star of the show."

I laughed loudly. "That's such a great story."

"That was the end of my drama career, incidentally."

"I'm not surprised," I said, still giggling.

Before long, we reached the periphery of a vivid green forest. A sign hung crookedly on one of the trees that read, 'Welcome to Nata. District under construction.'

"Should we be on a construction site?" I asked hesitantly.

Noah laughed at me. "You're so cautious... It's sweet. I'm not taking you anywhere dangerous, I promise."

"Ok," I said reluctantly. "I trust you." As I followed him into the trees, I started to feel a little strange. Not quite dizzy, but kind of light headed. It was becoming difficult to walk and I was worried I was going to faint.

"Oh, I should have warned you," Noah said with a twinkle in his eyes. "The gravitational pull is lower in Nata. Don't worry, you're not going to pass out. Maybe just try and bounce a bit instead of walking like you usually would."

I did as I was told and he was right, it was much easier to walk this way. Less like I was wading through a muddy swamp, more like I was walking on a trampoline. I followed Noah to the opposite side of the wood and as the trees cleared, a kind of adventure playground came into view. Climbing frames, poles, bars and handles had been fabricated from timber logs, and natural wood chips dusted the floor.

"Watch this." Noah bent his knees and then almost dove into the air. He kicked his legs and then spun around, to catch my expression, floating in the air as if he were treading water.

My jaw might as well have been on the floor. "You're flying," I said, frozen to the spot and unable to articulate what I could see.

Noah laughed. "Try it. Just push off the ground and then move your body like you're swimming." I shook my head in horror. "Ok, maybe just bounce around for a bit then, until you get used to it."

Noah swam off to the climbing frames and began swinging himself around like an acrobat, letting me bob about awkwardly without him watching. I allowed myself to get further off the ground with each step until finally I gave a little kick and suddenly I was flying. I was *actually* flying. I floated around, kicking my legs every now and then to keep myself off the ground. I found myself laughing and caught Noah's eye who was watching me with a wide smile on his face. My confidence grew and I began to push myself further upwards, passing the climbing frames and the trees. Within moments, I felt a shift in the atmosphere and I abruptly began to drift unintentionally upwards. I looked around for something to grab onto, but I'd somehow flown too high. The planet's gravitational pull was quickly disappearing and I suddenly found myself headed towards the skies and out of control.

Chapter 12

I glanced down at my feet to see the ground drifting steadily further away and I quickly averted my gaze. I was just starting to quietly panic when Noah swooped into view and grabbed both of my hands. He tugged firmly, pulling me down, and we started to gravitate towards the ground. As soon as I felt the wood chippings beneath my feet, relief flooded through my veins. I stood there motionlessly, both of my hands still resting in Noah's, and before I knew what was happening, Noah's mouth was on mine. His lips lingered for no longer than a heart beat, and then he was gone. I spun around to see him swinging around on the climbing frame and my relief was very quickly replaced by confusion and then fury. I stormed over to him with great difficulty and then stood with my hands on my hips. He saw my expression and almost flinched. He stopped swinging and came over to me with a look of concern mixed with guilt in his eyes.

"Are you ok?" he asked quietly.

"No thanks to you!" I fumed. "You promised you wouldn't take me anywhere dangerous. Who knows what could have happened if you hadn't reached me in time?"

"But I did reach you in time," Noah said looking bewildered. "I was watching you the whole time. I never would have let anything happen to you."

I was so angry that I could hardly speak. He shouldn't have let it happen in the first place. Or at least warned me not to go so high.

"I want to go home," I said, suddenly needing to be anywhere but there.

"Ok… Well, I'll get the cap sent over then." He pressed some buttons on his watch and then, downhearted, started to move off in the direction of the station. I followed him from a safe distance with my arms crossed.

We swiped our watches at the cap port and both climbed in silently. Neither of us spoke for the duration of the journey home. I sat with my back to Noah the whole way, looking resolutely out of the window, even though there was nothing to see but endless tubing. The cap stopped at my home first and Noah touched my arm as I got out. "I'm sorry, Mia."

He looked crushed, but I couldn't find the right words to say. I mumbled goodbye and quickly exited the capsule, stumbling into the house through the garage door. I stood with my back against the door, the anger replaced with a sad sort of emptiness. GG wasn't home so I managed to get to my bedroom without having to make polite conversation. I couldn't have handled that.

I passed the kitchen table and picked up some mail addressed to me. There were two letters. One was in a pink envelope addressed in sparkly purple pen. I didn't need to check the return address, I'd know Ellie's loopy lettering anywhere. And the other was in a thick white envelope, marked in my mum's sharp black print. I took them both to my room and lay on my stomach to read them. I couldn't face reading what my mum had to say, so I opted for the safety of Ellie's letter first.

To my long lost friend, Mia

I am missing you terribly! I feel like I have lost a sister. I have done nothing but grieve for you these past few weeks. Life will never be the same. It is a travesty that you have left.

I feel like I'm in a Jane Austen story, having to write to you like this - we're studying her at school this semester. Why oh why do you not have the internet?! I don't think I could live without it.

I have begged my parents incessantly since you left, and I think I've finally convinced them to let me visit you once I turn sixteen. Only about a year to wait then. Do you think you'll come back for a visit before then? Please say yes!

In other news, the love of your life, Jack has moved swiftly on and is dating that horrible Amber girl from the year below us. He clearly has no taste so you had a lucky escape there.

It is utterly freezing here – I am so jealous that you are somewhere warm and sunny and I am stuck here in some kind of wintery hell.

As you well know, it will be my fifteenth birthday very soon… One step closer to adulthood and freedom. My parents are actually letting me throw a party for the first time ever. I think they're trying to cheer me up as I've been quite a grump since you left. But of course you won't be there, and I will be miserable without you.

Miss you more than words can say. Write back quickly! I can't wait to hear all about your New Mexican adventures.

Love you lots
Your best friend forever
Ellie xxx

I put down the letter and wiped the salty water from my cheeks. They had started off as tears of laughter but as the reality of the situation dawned on me, they quickly became real tears of deep sadness. I'd been blocking everything from my mind, refusing to think about how far away from home I was, and how I might never see my friends and family again. For the first time, I really let myself cry. It had started to go dark by the time my eyes dried up and I finally felt capable of opening the letter from my mum. I picked it up cautiously and her scent drifted into my consciousness. My throat tightened at the familiar, calming smell and I could feel my eyes well up again. I ripped open the envelope and sat up to read the letter.

My darling daughter, Mia

I am unbelievably sorry it has taken me so long to write. I thought it seemed the most sensible idea at the time - allowing you to settle in, without thinking of home. In retrospect, perhaps it wasn't the best idea I've had.

Your great grandfather tells me you seem quite at home and have made a few friends already. I knew it would suit you there. I hope you understand why I thought it would be good for you at the time. Of course, you probably won't see it from my point of view, you have always been stubborn, just like me.

You might have already heard, the conflict I was sent to follow in the Middle East seems to have calmed down for now. So I've been sent back home for the time being.

The weather is just awful here and everyone is in post-Christmas hibernation. You are not missing a thing. The house is so lonely without you, it seems to rattle and creak all the time, which I'd never noticed before.

I'm sure you're having a wonderful time and haven't given home a second thought… But if you did decide you wanted to come home, I would really love to have you back. My heart just aches when I think about how far away you are and I miss you more than I could ever have imagined. All you have to do is say the word.

All my love
Mum xxx

I didn't think it was possible to cry any more, but I seemed to manage it. Deep, powerful sobs that made my rib cage ache. Suddenly, I didn't want to have to make vital life changing decisions for the entire planet, or only eat food that my body needed, instead of what I felt like eating. I just wanted a greasy burger and French fries and a block of milk chocolate. One of those giant ones. I wanted to sit around in front of the TV in my pyjamas, with the quilt over me. I wanted to look outside of the window in the morning and be surprised by the weather. But most of all, I wanted my mum, my dad and Ellie. I finally understood the term 'homesickness'. I actually felt sick to my stomach with longing for my home on Earth. All I had to do was say the word. And at that moment, I knew. It was time to go home.

I awoke early the next day after a fitful sleep. I crept into the kitchen and found GG reading the Sunday paper. He looked up and concern immediately spread across his brow.

"What's the matter, dear?" he asked, lowering the paper.

I slunk into the seat opposite him and clasped my hands together uneasily. "I had a letter from Mum yesterday..." I started.

GG looked at me knowingly, as if he could anticipate what was coming. "How is Miranda?"

"She's, well... She says she's lonely... And she'd like me to come home. If I wanted to." I looked down at my hands.

"And do you want to?"

I looked up and nodded. I couldn't speak then for fear of crying.

"I know how you're feeling, Mia... I went through exactly the same thing when I arrived on Usonia, all those years ago." He put down the paper and placed a hand over mine. "I remember how hard it was leaving my wife and children, and having to lie to them about it. That made it so much worse, somehow."

I smiled tearily at GG, still unable to speak.

"But how could I refuse the opportunity to serve my country and help save the human race? I was chosen, and I couldn't turn it down. How could anyone turn that down? But, slowly, I made new friends and found new loved ones. We built new families and communities. Before long, Usonia had become home. It will become home for you too, child."

I nodded so that he knew I understood, but a sob caught in my throat and I began to cry. GG stood up and slid into the seat next to me, placing his arm around my shoulder.

"Now, now, there's no need for tears. If you really want to go home, I won't stop you. I understand."

I nodded vigorously and wiped my eyes, trying to catch my breath.

"Would you like me to make the arrangements for you?"

I nodded again. "Please."

"Then consider it done."

I couldn't face the prospect of more goodbyes so I turned down the offer of a farewell party. GG, Priscilla, Stella and Noah all saw me to the space station but I could barely look anyone in the eye. I didn't think I could possibly have any tears left in me, but I didn't want to test it.

Noah pulled me to one side. "This isn't because of me is it? You're not leaving because of me?" He looked genuinely worried.

"Of course not. It was just an accident. I miss home, that's all. I promise."

Noah breathed a sigh of relief. "So we're friends?"

"Of course we're friends." I smiled reassuringly. Noah gave me a quick hug and then stood back for the others to have their turn.

Stella sobbed and gripped me tightly. I was worried she wasn't going to let go of me for a minute. Priscilla kissed me on both cheeks and wished me luck. And then GG stood before me. We looked at each other sadly. I was so full of emotion that I couldn't speak, my throat was all choked up. GG held me tightly without saying a word. He didn't have to.

I boarded the ship alone, without turning back. I didn't think I could see their faces without breaking down.

Chapter 13

I hardly remember anything of the journey back to Earth. I spent most of it sleeping or staring numbly at the wall. Pamela and Dylan both gave me a wide berth, occasionally checking that I was ok or bringing food to my room. I avoided the anti gravity playroom as if it led to the black hole.

On landing, I was greeted by a new military escort. I was relieved about that. I couldn't have faced pretending to be cheerful for Lieutenant Marshall. The flight seemed short in comparison to the space trip and I must have stared out of the window into nothingness for the entire journey. The man in the seat next to me tried to make polite conversation but he dropped it when he didn't get any response.

My mum was there to greet me at the arrivals gate, her eyes watering up at the sight of me, and she threw her arms around me. We held each other tightly, not wanting to let go. Eventually, she stepped back and smoothed my hair away from my face, as if checking I was the same person that had left.

"You look different," she said, almost accusingly.

"You look the same," I said, secretly glad she hadn't changed.

She took my bags from me and led me in the direction of the car.

I stepped outside, through the automatic doors, to be met by an assaulting smell. A sort of dirty, metallic vapour crawled up my nostrils and invaded my lungs. I started coughing instantly. I caught sight of the offender and shielded my mouth and nose with my arm. Thick, black smoke was spewing out of taxis, buses and cars, all lined up, waiting for passengers. Mum looked at me, surprised by my reaction and then had to hurry after me as I started jogging towards the car.

It was the same car she'd had for years, but I'd never noticed how ugly it was before now. It was long and angular, once silver but now a dull murky colour that resembled dust. It looked like a gnarly rhino.

The car started with a grating snarl and it made me jump. I looked out of the window as we jerkily left the car park and pulled out onto the tarmac road. Heavy raindrops bounced off the puddles of murky water that filled the numerous pot holes scattered across the roads. I looked up to see low, gloomy clouds smothering the entire sky and in the distance, factory buildings lined the horizon. As soon as we hit the motorway we came to a standstill. I looked at the congested roads. Rows and rows of vehicles crawled across the ground, moving slower than I could walk on my hands and knees. I knew my mum could tell I wasn't in the mood for conversation and she turned on the radio.

After a few dreary and inane songs, a monotone male voice began to read the news. It announced that the new government was planning to cut spending on schooling and healthcare.

I frowned. "If the population carries on growing, and the government keeps making cuts to spending on schools and healthcare, how does that work?" I asked, the first words I'd uttered in about an hour.

"It doesn't, darling, it doesn't," my mum said, looking at me curiously. "Since when did you start taking an interest in politics?"

"Oh, we study it at my new school."

The newsreader switched to local news. Gun shots had been fired late last night in the next town to ours.

"I don't understand why guns are even legal. Drugs are banned almost everywhere on the planet, but people can have guns? It doesn't make any sense!"

"I couldn't agree more, darling." My mum had a funny expression on her face, almost like she was proud.

More news spat out from the distorted speakers and I listened with a sickness in my stomach. A fifteen year old girl had been assaulted outside our corner shop in broad daylight. An elderly neighbour had been broken into and had her jewellery box stolen, full of sentimental, irreplaceable possessions. A nineteen year old boy had been punched and killed trying to break up a fight in a park. A local teenager had committed suicide after being repeatedly bullied at school. The school *I* used to go to. A four year old girl had been abducted from her own back garden yesterday afternoon. How had I been so blind when I lived here? My memory of Earth was of this beautiful, harmonious place. But now I could see it all so clearly. Our species was destroying itself and the very planet it occupies. It was devastating.

We arrived at the house after hours of being stuck in the car. I couldn't believe it could take so long to travel just 60 kilometres. That would have taken around fifteen minutes on Usonia. My dad told me that we only get an average of 650,000 hours in a life time. Just think how many of those are wasted just sitting in traffic or waiting for a bus. It was depressing.

We walked past the bare trees lining the driveway, silhouetted against the twilight sky. They reminded me of witches bent double, claws poised to reach out and grab passing children. I walked quickly down the driveway, reaching the porch as Mum was jiggling the lock, letting the door swing open as she threw my bags inside.

I stepped over the luggage and squeezed in through the hallway. I walked from room to room, amazed at how dark and poky the place was. I'd thought I'd had it pretty good, but the house seemed tiny now. My room was practically a shoe box. I opened my wardrobe and eyed my old clothes. They seemed garish in comparison to the ones on Usonia. I tried on one of my old favourite tops and it crackled over my hair and then clung to my skin with static. It fitted a little too snugly and I checked myself in the mirror. I definitely wasn't overweight, I just looked healthy now, more athletic looking.

I felt horrible after the long journey so I had a quick shower and then towel dried my hair. It sprung up almost instantly, all wiry and fluffy. Nothing seemed to suit me on Earth. First the air, now the water... I was already worried about the climate. It was somewhere between freezing and warm outside, but it just felt like a kind of dull nothingness. Inside, the heating was on full and it was making my skin dry out already.

I got dressed into the loosest clothes I could find and then walked downstairs. I went past the lounge where my mum was sat in front of the television with a glass of wine and a large block of chocolate. In the kitchen, I opened the pantry to find bags of fatty crisps, packs of dehydrated noodles, and assorted packets of sweets and chocolate, all full of mysterious ingredients that began with the letter E. How could people bear to put all this stuff into their bodies without knowing what it was? I looked at my watch and then realised it was pretty much useless here. How would I know what nutrients my body needed without it? Suddenly I was glad I'd paid attention in our nutrition classes at school. I checked the fridge and freezer but they were full of processed foods. There didn't seem to be anything of nutritional value in the house. I remember Mum used to cook before Dad left, but since then, we'd lived off a diet of ready meals. I settled for baked beans on toast rather than risk a frozen processed meal and resolved to go to the farmers' market later the next day.

I slept fitfully that night, kept awake by the glare of the streetlights and the growl of cars as they roared past at all hours. I awoke early the next morning and slunk out of bed to peer through the curtains. The skies were gun metal grey and cast a dismal shadow across the ground. I got dressed quickly and then glanced in the mirror. My face was already erupting in spots just from eating that white bread last night, and my stomach was all swollen in objection. I went down to the kitchen and started to prepare breakfast, before realising the eggs were from a battery farm. Suddenly I didn't feel hungry anymore. I wrote a note for my mum who was still in bed and then snuck out, hazarding the harsh February air to meet Ellie in town.

I arrived at the bus stop with a couple of minutes to spare, only to see the bus pulling off just as I reached it. I checked the time table and saw that there was another one due in ten minutes. I hopped around to keep warm, breathing on my hands to heat them. After around fifteen minutes a bus flew past, overflowing with people standing in the aisle. My heart sank and my forced optimism was beginning to wane. The next bus was due in five minutes but it didn't arrive for another fifteen. By the time I boarded, my teeth were chattering and I couldn't feel my ears anymore.

The bus chugged along, stopping and starting every two minutes, travelling at an average speed of around eight kilometres an hour. I could feel my entire body tensing the longer I sat there. Eventually we pulled up at the central station and I practically leapt off the bus. I barrelled my way towards the shopping centre, trying not to look at the concrete pavements speckled with chewing gum and smeared with dog faeces. Cigarette buts littered the ground and plastic bags and crisp packets whipped around in the wind, softly screeching along the paving slabs like finger nails against glass.

I walked past an old homeless man sat shivering in a doorway. He asked if I could spare any change but I didn't have the right currency in my purse and it made me feel wretched. I didn't understand how our governments could let this kind of thing happen. A warm and safe place to lay your head was a basic human right, surely. It was inhumane making people beg for their survival.

I let out a sigh of relief as I reached the warmth of the mall. I stepped in through the sliding doors and then almost reeled back in alarm. Crowds of people roamed the centre in total chaos. I shoved my way in and headed in the direction of my old favourite coffee shop. I pushed past acne-ridden obese people with lank greasy hair, carrying paper bags loaded with fast food. Mums that couldn't be a day over fifteen pushing toddlers in buggies - mobile phone in one hand and jumbo can of sickly sweet energy drink in the other.

Gangs of teenage boys yelling abuse at shoppers as they passed by. I couldn't believe I used to spend almost all of my weekends here. I couldn't wait to get out. I put my head down and hurried on.

As the coffee shop came into view, I charged forward, narrowly missing a head-on collision with a couple crossing my path.

I stopped to apologise and then realised that I was face to face with Jack Faraday. He was taller than I remembered and he'd filled out a little, but he had the same dimpled cheeks, mop of unruly black hair and green eyes that always seemed to twinkle with amusement.

"Mia!" Jack's face broke into a broad smile. "You look incredible…"

"Jack… hi. Wow, you've really grown since December. I almost didn't recognise you…"

Amber nudged him with her elbow.

"You remember Amber? From school?"

"Of course, hi Amber…"

She smiled politely while Jack stood there beaming at me.

"Well, I've got to run, I'm supposed to be meeting Ellie and I'm already late."

"Oh, ok, well, it was really great seeing you, Mia, really great."

I waved goodbye and hurried in the direction of the coffee shop, reaching it at record speed.

I squeezed through the hoards and found Ellie at our usual table. Her face broke into a huge grin as she saw me and she leapt out of her seat, spilling her drink and elbowing the man at the neighbouring table in the head in the process.

"Oops, sorry... Mia! I'm so happy to see you!" She threw her arms around me and rocked me from side to side until I almost tipped over and then we fell apart laughing. "I already got your drink - your old favourite." She pushed a mug towards me, slopping hot chocolate all over the table. Synthetic whipped cream dribbled down the sides and marshmallows bobbed about on top. My stomach turned at the thought of it.

"Oh... Thank you!" I didn't want to be ungrateful so I smiled and listened to Ellie's news while surreptitiously picking out the marshmallows and hiding them in a napkin.

Ellie looked at me like I had some kind of mental problem and said, "Mia, what are you doing?"

"Oh... Um... Well, I've been studying nutrition in New Mexico and I found out some gross things about marshmallows. And squirty cream, really." I spooned the cream out of the cup and onto the napkin.

"What did you find out?" she asked suspiciously.

"Squirty cream is basically just a lot of sugar and gas, and marshmallows are made from the bits of animals that nobody else wants," I said, grimacing at the visual in my head.

"Shut up! That's not true."

"It is, actually."

"Whatever… Anyway, tell me about New Mexico! You look amazing! Love the tan." She ate one of the marshmallows from her own hot chocolate.

"New Mexico is… great. The weather is beautiful all the time. My school is really interesting and the teachers are so nice. My great grandfather is pretty cool, even though he's about a hundred years old… The people are super friendly. I've made a couple of good friends – they're called Stella and Noah." My heart twisted at the thought of them.

"So why the hell are you back?" she asked, slurping her hot chocolate noisily.

"For you, of course!" I laughed and she grinned back at me. "Tell me *everything* I've missed."

"Where do I begin?! Well, I told you about Jack didn't I? He started seeing Amber almost straight after you left. She's totally vile, a complete troll…"

"I just bumped into them actually. I thought she was quite sweet."

"Well now she's dating the love of your life and so of course we hate her," she said, looking at me as if I was stupid. She carried on, "Jack is failing absolutely everything by the way, did you know he was so dumb? I had no idea…"

My eyes started to glaze over at this barrage of negativity, and I could feel my temples tightening. "Actually, Ellie, I'm starting to feel really sick, I think I'm going to have to go home."

"Oh." She looked disappointed. "You do kind of look unwell, now you mention it. Are you ok?"

"It's probably jetlag. I just need to go home and rest."

"Ok… There's a half price sale on at Angel. You're sure you don't want to come and check it out?"

"I really need to get home, Ellie, I'm sorry." I scraped back my chair, hugged her goodbye and fled out of the shop.

I rammed my way through the crowds, crossing the street to avoid a group of men in baseball caps holding cans of lager. They shouted something vulgar but I carried on looking straight ahead, pretending I couldn't hear them. There was a long, winding queue when I reached the bus stop. The woman in front of me was holding a cigarette in her hand and the smoke billowed in my face. The smell made me want to vomit and I started coughing involuntarily. The woman looked at me like I was dirt, as if my cough was passing judgement on her.

I felt a drop of rain land on the bridge of my nose and I became aware that the streets had noticeably darkened. More rain drops began to splatter my face and then suddenly the clouds burst and icy rain came lashing down. I looked around for shelter, but there was nothing. I optimistically checked my bag for an umbrella but I knew I wouldn't have thought to pack it that morning. I'd been conditioned by Usonia's predictable weather system already.

There was nothing else to do but wait in the cold rain for the bus to arrive. Of course it was even later than usual because people didn't seem to be able to drive in the rain, so all traffic came to a standstill. The journey back took an eternity, and I sat there sopping wet and shivering. By the time I reached the house, my feet squelching with every step, I was sneezing and coughing like I had pneumonia.

I peeled off my clothes and stood under the hot shower, my skin tingling from the temperature change. As I stood there, the hot water bouncing off my head and shoulders, I started to wonder what I was doing there. I didn't really feel like I fitted in on Earth anymore. The more I thought about it, the more it became clear that Usonia was where I belonged .

I dried off, threw on a dressing gown and then picked up the phone to call my dad. It went straight to the answer service and my dad's voice came through the ear piece. The message said he was travelling internationally for the next fortnight and wouldn't be contactable until his return. I was devastated, I really wanted to see him before I left. This time it would be for good, and the thought of not seeing my dad ever again made my heart break.

My mum came home early that day and called for me as soon as she entered the house. I came down the stairs to find her sitting on the sofa with her head in her hands. I sat down next to her and put my arm gingerly around her shoulders. "Is everything ok, Mum?"

She sat up and looked at me with pain in her eyes. "It's your great grandfather... He's been taken into hospital; they don't know if he's going to make it."

Chapter 14

"GG?" My eyes flooded with water instantly and my chest contracted with anguish. My mum nodded miserably and we hugged each other tightly. We stayed like that for a really long time, until neither of us could cry any more, and we felt strong enough to let go.

"Mum," I said slowly, "I think I want to go back. I want to be with GG."

"Of course you do, darling." She smiled, tears shining in her eyes.

"Can't you come too?"

"My home is here sweetheart. My whole life is here. You understand, don't you?"

"I understand." I nodded sadly.

"I'll sort out the travel arrangements now. You go and get some rest; you look tired. I'll see you in the morning." She kissed me on the forehead and I sloped off to bed.

We managed to get flights for the next day. Everything happened so fast that I didn't even get around to unpacking, so getting ready to leave again took no time at all. Ellie came with us to the airport and she just sat there silently, holding my hand. I stared out of the window, biting on my lip. There was no physical way I could get to Usonia any faster but I was still tensed, as if I could speed up the process by sheer force of will. I didn't want to even consider the possibility that GG might be gone by the time I got there. Mum and Ellie waved me off at the departure gate and I hurried through, not wanting to delay the trip by even a second.

I couldn't concentrate at all on the flight. I put in my earphones, purely to deter strangers from talking to me. I held a book in my lap throughout the journey, occasionally letting my eyes cast over the words, but I wasn't taking anything in. Sometimes I'd turn the page without noticing that I hadn't actually read a word of the previous one.

I was ushered onto the jet plane and then straight onto the standing spaceship. There was a new crew this time, and I didn't bother making polite conversation. I bit my finger nails and paced around a lot during the three day space trip. Finally we landed and I practically threw myself out of the ship. Priscilla was there to greet me and she looked emotionally drained.

"I am so sorry about your great grandfather, darling, it must have been a horrible shock for you." She gave me a hug but I extricated myself after a couple of seconds.

"Can you take me to him? I need to see him."

"Of course." She took one of my bags from me and we both picked up speed, hurrying towards the Hyper Transport Interchange.

The cap took us straight to the hospital. It was the first time I'd been there but I was too anxious to take in my surroundings. Priscilla offered to take my luggage back to the house, while I was ushered towards GG's room. The nurse left me at the doorway and I stood there quietly, watching him sleep. His skin reminded me of crepe paper and his breathing was ragged and hoarse. He looked more old and frail than the last time I'd seen him, but peaceful somehow.

I crept into the room and sat down next to his bed, taking his hand into my own. I didn't want to disturb him, so I sat in silence, just relieved to be near him. Once my breathing had slowed and my heart had stopped thudding in my chest, I finally felt that I could take my eyes off GG and look around me. It was like we were in a strange sort of futuristic sanctuary. Like some kind of hybrid of a spa and an air traffic control tower. The monitors and charts were all displayed electronically on wall-mounted, clear glass screens. The lights were dimmed to allow GG to rest, but the effect was warm and calming. The colour scheme was neutral and everything was made from natural fabrics and materials. Soft, soothing music played in the background and aromatherapy oils burned around the room. I felt more relaxed just having been in there for five minutes.

It was easy to lose track of time in that room so I had no idea how long I'd been there when GG started to stir. His eyes fluttered and then blinked, adjusting to the low light. Gradually he registered my presence and the corners of his mouth upturned in a weak smile. My mood lifted instantly.

"GG!" I whispered. "I've never been so happy to see you."

"Mia... Is it really you? I'm not dreaming?" he asked hoarsely.

"It's really me. I got on the next flight the minute I heard. Are you ok?"

"I'm alright, just about. I'm not in any pain, I'm just tired. And so very weak. Even the simplest task seems a tremendous effort now."

"What happened, GG?"

"It was a heart attack. Only a mild one. The old ticker pulled through on its own, which was lucky. I wouldn't still be here otherwise."

"What do you mean?" I asked, frowning.

GG took a deep raspy breath. "We don't bring the dead back to life on Usonia."

"I still don't understand."

"Have you heard of DNR?"

I shook my head.

"It stands for, 'Do Not Resuscitate. It means once any of your organs fail, they fail for good. It means it's your time to go." He took another deep, painful-sounding breath, while I sat there in silence trying to process his words. "We do everything we can to live long, happy, healthy lives, but we don't believe in trying to cheat death. My heart is still going for now, but the doctors have told me it will fail again soon, and when it does, they won't revive me. I haven't got long left, Mia."

"How can you be so calm about this?" I choked. "I'm not ready to lose you yet; I only just found you!" I clung onto his hand tighter until I could see him wince in pain.

"Darling, of course I'm hurting for you. Please don't be sad. It's the natural order of things. We all have to die some time, and I've reached my time. When the pain gets too much to bear, the doctor will come and end it for me."

"End it?" My chest started to hurt. I had some idea what he meant by those words, but I didn't wanted to admit it to myself.

"When I'm ready, I will call for the doctor and he will administer an injection. I'll fall quickly into unconsciousness, like a deep peaceful sleep. Only I won't ever wake up. It's the most serene and humane way to die. You don't need to be afraid for me."

I was suddenly finding it very difficult to breathe and my face felt like it was burning. I wanted to speak but no words would come out.

"Come now, dear. Enough of this morbid talk. Save your tears for the funeral; I'm not dead yet." He patted my hand with an understanding smile. "Now, tell me about your visit home."

I took a wavering breath. "It was... horrible. Just horrible. I felt so sad being there. There are so many atrocities happening all around the world and nobody seems to be doing anything about it. The human race really does need to be saved, but not from some distant threat of nuclear war. From itself."

GG must have been able to read the anguish in my expression because he squeezed my hand tight.

"Is there really no way we can start rescuing people on Earth sooner than planned? Without compromising the wellbeing of Usonia?" I asked desperately.

GG looked at me with sorrow in his eyes. "Without compromising the planet and its people? I really don't believe it can be done. Not right away anyway." He looked thoughtful for a moment. "Although... Perhaps if we increased the population, just slightly, then maybe we could speed up construction without damaging the planet. That might appease Conan too."

I'd been so wrapped up in my own problems that I'd forgotten all about Conan. "How did your meeting go last week?" I asked guiltily.

GG sighed. "He issued an ultimatum. Final talks with the government officials take place on Usonia next week and if we can't come to a friendly agreement, he has threatened to stage a global presidential intervention. I'm afraid that if that happens, we'll lose absolutely everything, and Usonia will become another Earth before we know it."

"I won't let that happen. I promise." I squeezed GG's hand again, more gently this time. He squeezed back lightly and then I felt his grip loosen.

I could see he was rapidly losing lucidity and he drifted fitfully into sleep. Seconds later, his eyes flicked open and he clutched his chest, gasping in agony. I leapt back in horror and looked around for a doctor or a nurse. People in white coats rushed into the room and a man started bathing GG's head with a flannel. His eyes weren't focusing, as if he'd gone blind with pain. I watched as the doctor picked up a syringe and began to fill it with a clear liquid.

I suddenly realised what was going on and I pushed forward, wrapping my arms around GG. "No! Please don't do this! You can't do this. He's my only family here. I need him." I turned to my great grandfather and stroked his head. "GG, please stay, please don't leave me," I pleaded futilely.

The nurse touched my elbow sympathetically. "Miss McAdams, it's time. Your great grandfather is in a lot of pain and we need to ease it for him. You need to let him go."

I began choking back sobs and water started to stream down my face. I held onto GG tightly for as long as the doctors let me. After another gentle nudge, I stepped back and fell into a chair, my chest heaving with sadness. I watched in agony as they swiftly administered the injection and at last he was truly at peace.

I stayed at the hospital until Priscilla came to pay her respects and then she took me home.

"Would you like me to come in with you?" she asked from the cap port.

I shook my head. "No, thank you."

She hugged me tightly and then watched me with worry in her eyes as I left the capsule. I gave her a small smile and a wave to let her know that I was ok, and then apprehensively walked into the house.

It felt strangely empty, even though it was really no different to normal. GG's coat, hat and silk scarf hung neatly on the coat rack and seeing it made my face contract in pain.

His breakfast sat unfinished beside an open newspaper on the kitchen table. I walked over to clear away the plates and glanced at the paper. An article about The Administration's most recent meeting with Earth officials stared back up at me. I froze, a glass of orange juice in one hand and a plate of barely touched scrambled eggs in the other. It felt like a knife had pierced my heart. GG must have been reading this when his heart attack came on. Not only was Conan trying to destroy Usonia, but he was now at least partially responsible for the death of my great grandfather. Some kind of fire engulfed my insides and my grief was replaced with a fury I had never felt before. It struck me like a bulldozer. GG had died before his life's mission was complete. He'd sacrificed *everything* for Project Ark. I couldn't allow it all to be ripped away by Conan. I knew then what I needed to do. Suddenly I understood why I had been sent to this planet. My great grandfather's mission was now mine. I would protect Usonia to the death, just as he had done.

Having a sense of purpose gave me the strength I needed to carry on. If I was going to join The Administration and stop Conan, I couldn't sit around feeling sorry for myself. School took on a strange new meaning. I knew it was helping me prepare for something big. Something important and real. Mr Kepler tried to send me home on my first day back but I stubbornly stayed put. Suddenly I was the most attentive person in class, and that's an accomplishment on Usonia.

GG's memorial service took place a week later. It seemed as though it was attended by every single person on Usonia, and the whole of Paramount City shut down for the day. It was held in a sprawling meadow on a mild, spring-like day. Everyone wore white, as was the tradition on Usonia, according to Stella, and the girls had colourful flowers pinned into their hair. A swing band played soft, cheerful music at the back of the field and everyone greeted each other with smiles and warmth. It was almost impossible to feel downhearted. Stella stood next to me and held my hand while streams of people came to tell me what a wonderful man my great grandfather was, and how full and accomplished his life was. Stella told me that it's not normal to mourn the dead on Usonia. Memorial services there were always a celebration of life.

Everyone took it in turns to stand at the front and share their memories of GG, and it was difficult not to smile. After everyone had spoken, the party relocated to the edge of a sparse young wood.

"This is the cemetery," Stella said quietly.

I looked around surprised. There were no tombs or head stones, just a scattering of youthful-looking trees. Some blossoming, some vivid green and flourishing. Wooden swings hung from some of the eldest trees, and ornate benches sat surrounded by plants and flowers. A crowd had gathered around a freshly dug hole in the ground and people respectfully watched while GG's body, wrapped in a cotton shroud, was carried on a wicker stretcher and lowered slowly into the ground.

"Where's the coffin?" I whispered to Stella.

"We don't have them here," she replied under her breath. "It allows the dead to decompose, to provide nutrients for nature. He'll be at one with the planet now. It's a beautiful, natural circle of life."

The crowd surged forward in turn to throw flowers into the grave. I carefully laid the last flower and then everyone stepped back to allow the hole to be filled with soil. The service ended with the planting of a young cherry blossom tree at the centre. Afterwards, everyone piled back to the house and the rest of the day was entirely consumed by hostess duties. It wasn't until the house had emptied that I finally allowed myself to grieve for my great grandfather. I sat down in his armchair and I wept.

Chapter 15

I arrived at school the next day to find my entire class milling around outside the front of the building, laughing and talking excitedly. I spotted Noah sat on a bench reading a book and I wandered over in his direction.

"What's going on?" I asked, sliding into the seat next to him.

He put down his book and smiled. "School trip. Didn't anyone tell you?"

"I have no idea. My mind has kind of been elsewhere this past week." I'd forgotten how striking he was, with his glowing bronze skin, thick, dishevelled hair and deep mesmerising eyes. I found it difficult to concentrate for a second.

"How are you holding up?" He looked at me searchingly. "Lonely in that big house of yours? You're always welcome at our place you know."

"Thank you, that's very sweet. I'm holding up ok, just about." I looked away to see Stella bounding over.

She flung herself onto the bench and beamed. "I'm so excited about today… I love school trips!"

Noah rolled his eyes discretely and then went back to his book. I struggled to supress a smile.

"Where are we actually going? This is all news to me," I asked Stella.

"To The Administration! It's our orientation day."

"Orientation day?" I asked, confused.

"We get a tour of The Administration building in preparation for when we all get to work there after school finishes…"

Mr Kepler interrupted our conversation before I could find out more. "Come on, class, this way to The Administration, follow me! No dawdling, we've got a busy day."

It was only a short walk to The Administration building and on arrival we were instantly greeted at the door by an overjoyed-looking Priscilla. "Welcome, future workers of The Administration!" she said beaming, her blonde locks shimmering in the sunlight. "Come on in and make yourselves right at home."

We all filed into a light, bright and airy room. It was circular, of course, with floor to ceiling infinity glazing looking out onto an expanse of green landscaping. Classical music played softly through speakers that were hidden around the room.

Priscilla noticed me looking at the secreted speakers and smiled. "Music to stimulate the mind," she said, gesturing towards the speakers, and then turned to face the main area of the office. "This half of the building is the main working hub. It's a totally flexible working space. No-one has their own desk and you can choose where you work depending on how you feel that day, or even at that minute."

I looked around the room to see bench-style desks and stools lining the windows. Further in sat boardroom-style tables, with workers bent over the built-in screens, deep in conversation. People were stood at standing desks, huddled around circular tables, lounging on sofas at coffee tables, or even working on picnic tables outside. Everywhere I turned, I was surrounded by young, attractive and productive-looking workers. It was not how I imagined any kind of government building to look.

A windowless interior room with glass screens built into its walls lay at the centre of the building. Priscilla pointed towards it. "These screens permanently broadcast the digital bulletin board and constantly track any suggestions for action or any complaints to proposals from the public. It automatically allocates anything that needs actioning to the next available administrator. Actions vary from simple implementation tasks, like a quick repair job, to the organisation of a public referendum. Behind the walls, you'll find our rest pod. It's important that the administrators are alert and fit to do their job, so we've made this room available for anyone that needs a power nap during the day. We've found it keeps everyone working at peak performance."

A sign above the door signalled that the room was unoccupied, and we were ushered into a space thick with darkness. Priscilla flicked a switch and the semi circular room slowly came into view. Low lighting spread across the floor, highlighting sumptuous-looking beds, all lined up along the wall.

"The beds are hooked up to sleep sensors and they're programmed to wake you up just before you hit the deep sleep cycle. That way there's no risk of anyone accidentally sleeping for half the day, which could easily be done in this room."

I looked around and privately agreed. I was feeling sleepy just standing in there.

As if she could read my mind, Priscilla added, "The pillows are scented with real lavender and chamomile to aid sleep and relaxation. No-one ever has any trouble falling asleep in here." She laughed. "Come on, let's get out of here before we all start feeling like it's time for a nap."

Priscilla led us back out and around to the opposite side of the inner circle. "Gentlemen, if you'd like to take the door to your left, I'll take the ladies into this one. We'll meet back out here." She pushed open the door to reveal a luxurious pamper room. There were mirrors, lounge-style seating, and shelves of natural fragrances and cosmetics along the back and left hand walls.

A row of doors lay to the right and Priscilla pointed to them one by one. "This door leads to the private massage therapy room. You can book the masseuse any time during working hours. These doors here lead to the toilets, baths and showers. It's really important to us that the working environment should be as comfortable as possible, promoting mental health as well as physical. We never seem to have any sick days here."

Next, we were ushered outside and around the back of the building. "Most of our recreational facilities are outside. We have a running track, lap pool, outdoor yoga studio and a multifunctional games court for tennis, volley ball, basket ball, soccer... You can also go for walks through the woods back there," she said, pointing. We all stood silent and still, utterly astounded. No wonder nobody turned down working at The Administration. It was like being paid to be at a holiday camp.

"Now I know what you must be thinking." Priscilla smiled. "When does anyone get any work done here? Well, the facilities are mostly used before and after work, and during break times, but people also use them for active meetings, or to inspire creativity. We actually found that productivity doubled once the recreational facilities were installed." Priscilla sat down at a large picnic table and motioned for us all to join her.

"Which brings me nicely to my next topic. You're probably wondering what to expect when you start working here. Well, the duties of the administrators are quite varied, which will make your weeks nice and interesting. One day you could be writing to Usonians, inviting them to carry out their administrative duty. Another day you might be issuing public notices about a proposal, or have to administer any increases or decreases to taxes. You might devise, issue and analyse our temperature checks, which are surveys that look at the overall happiness of the population of Usonia. You'll be implementing plans, hiring and paying contractors, maintaining databases of inhabitants... No day will ever be the same at The Administration. Did anyone have any questions?"

I raised my hand tentatively. "Isn't this building a little extravagant for a government office? Since it's paid for and maintained by tax payers' money... If this was on Earth, there would be an outcry."

Priscilla smiled at me. "That's a good point. You're right, on Earth it would be seen as excessive. On Usonia, everyone has the right and opportunity to work for The Administration. So it's a workplace for everyone. As the government administration, we should be setting the standard for workplaces everywhere on the planet. We want all workplaces to promote wellbeing, health, happiness, creativity and productivity, and so we lead by example. But of course, the people *are* the government on Usonia. The proposal went to public vote and Usonians voted in favour of the plans. Any other questions?"

Al piped up, "Where do people eat here?"

Priscilla sounded like a wind chime when she laughed. "Excellent question. Let's carry on with the tour then. Follow me!"

The tour continued into the kitchen garden, brimming with fruit, salad, herbs and vegetables. Goats and chickens roamed freely around the picnic tables.

"Anyone can help themselves to fruit and veggies throughout the day. Like I said, a healthy, happy workforce is important here. Just don't forget to program it into your watches!"

Al picked an apple from the tree and bit into it hungrily. We followed Priscilla through double doors and into the kitchen to see rows of automatic cookers lining the bench tops, with dishwashers and fridges lined up beneath. A manual food preparation area sat semi-neglected in the corner and a huge farmhouse-style table divided the kitchen from the lunch room. On the opposite side of the table were couches, coffee tables, and shelves decorated with games and musical instruments.

"So this is the kitchen, as I'm sure you can see for yourselves," Priscilla said, sweeping her arm around the room, "and over here we have the lunch room and break out space. It gets pretty sociable and rowdy at lunch time, as you can imagine… and then, down at the opposite side of the building, we have all the meeting rooms."

We followed her away from the lunch room, traipsing after her noisily. As we approached the meeting spaces, Priscilla turned around and put her finger to her lips. "We'll need to be quiet in this area," she whispered. "There are important interplanetary talks happening all this week, and there's a meeting happening in that room right now." As she nodded towards the door, it swung open as if on cue, and Priscilla uttered in a hushed voice, "Oh no, it's Conan."

Rage bubbled up inside me at the sound of his name and I whipped around to face my arch nemesis in the flesh. Standing in the doorway was a slim man of average height. He had neatly trimmed salt and pepper hair and grey eyes the colour of a stormy sea. He stood frozen in front of the door, his eyes locked on mine. And then he spoke.

"Mia?"

My voice came out as a croak. "Dad?"

Chapter 16

I was overwhelmed with conflicting emotions. The man I held accountable for my great grandfather's death, the man trying to destroy the only place I'd truly belonged... That man was my dad? A man whose beliefs and ideals I thought were my own? The man I'd loved more than words could ever convey? The two just didn't match up. It didn't make any sense.

"Wait right here, Mia," my dad said in an unfamiliar, commanding tone. He went back into the meeting room, said a few words to his colleagues, and then promptly returned. "I think it's about time everyone broke for lunch. Priscilla, do you mind if I take Mia off your hands for an hour? I think we've got a few things to discuss."

"Of course not, Con', I mean, ahem, Daniel." Priscilla blushed.

I stood as still as a sculpture while my dad marched off towards the exit. He turned back as he reached the door and beckoned for me to follow. Priscilla gave me a little shove and I walked hesitantly towards the door.

Neither of us spoke once we got outside. Dad pushed on, heading towards the woodland, and started hunting out a trail for us to follow. After a while he dropped back so we were walking side by side.

"So... How was New Mexico?"

I looked up sheepishly but didn't say a word.

He glanced at me with knowing eyes and then allowed us to walk in silence for a few more minutes before speaking again. "It must have been a surprise bumping into me here."

"*That's* the understatement of the century," I retorted and then snapped my mouth back shut firmly.

Dad laughed. "Oh Mia, it's so good to see you."

I scowled at him. "I don't even know who you are! You've *lied* to me for almost my *entire* life!"

"You lied too..."

"I had to!"

"So did I, Mia." He looked at me earnestly.

I sulked, but I knew he was right. We pressed on, rambling through the forest together in silence.

"I must say, I was as surprised to see you here, Mia."

I stopped for breath, propping my hands on my hips for support. "Yeah, it's a long story."

"And you're happy here? You look well. You seem… different." He analysed my face. "Healthier."

"I love it here. I really love it. It must be the most beautiful place in the universe." And then my face clouded over. "But you're trying to destroy it."

He frowned. "I'm not trying to *destroy* it, Mia. I'm trying to end this apartheid between the planets. I'm trying to stop the protective, nationalistic bigotry that is happening under your own nose. Usonians are living a privileged, elitist lifestyle on a practically empty planet, while millions are suffering on Earth. Do you think that's fair?"

I was stunned into silence.

"All I've ever stood for is freedom, choice, equality and honesty. The people of Earth no longer have that. We need to stop the lies. Stop the segregation. Now, before it's too late."

I was horrified. None of those ideas had even crossed my mind. I pushed off ahead, allowing myself time to collect my thoughts. My dad followed closely behind. He didn't speak, knowing I needed the time to process what he'd said.

After we'd walked for some time, we reached a tree that had fallen across our path. I sat down on the trunk, exhausted, and my dad followed suit.

We were both silent for a while and then I spoke slowly, trying to carefully articulate all the thoughts that were whirring around in my head.

"I honestly hadn't looked at it that way." I felt heart broken. It was as if I'd discovered Usonia was my evil fairy tale stepmother, and beneath all that superficial beauty, lay an ugly witch.

My dad looked relieved. "I'm so glad you see it my way. If only we could convince all the other Usonians that we need to stop all of this eco nonsense and start ramping up construction... Although with any luck, by the end of this week, we won't have to convince anyone on this planet of anything."

"What do you mean?" I asked nervously.

"If we can't come to a mutual agreement over the next couple of days, presidents from all over Earth will intervene and we'll reassume control of Usonia."

"No!" The scream was out of my mouth before I'd had chance to think. My dad looked at me, stunned, and the words just tumbled out of my mouth. "That would completely undermine Usonia's political system. The people of this planet are their own rulers. Everyone from the age of eleven has rights, responsibilities and privileges that people on Earth wouldn't even dream of. It's a system that has resulted in political harmony since humans first landed here in the 1950s. It's a system that could solve a huge chunk of the world's problems if it was introduced on Earth. Don't take that away from us. Don't take that away from the entire human race."

My dad stared at me in shock. He was silent for a while, considering what I'd said.

"But how will we get the Usonians to agree to forgo their ecological ideals so that we can speed up construction on the planet and prepare for mass inhabitation?"

"You won't. Usonians are educated on sustainability, ecology, nutrition and politics from an early age. There's no way they would agree to harming the planet in exchange for interplanetary equality. And neither would I. There has to be another way."

My dad looked surprised. "You never struck me as the hippy type. I never would have thought you'd believe in all this airy fairy, greenie rubbish."

I stood up and turned to face my dad in exasperation. "Caring for the planet isn't about protecting nature so that we can all hug trees, hold hands and sing hymns. It's not about preserving the planet for future generations - nobody really cares whether our decedents have oil or trees hundreds of years down the line. Humans are far too selfish and short sighted. Nor is it about some contentious idea that the damage we're causing is bringing about climate change." I took a breath. "It's about keeping the air we breathe clean so that there's less sickness on the planet. So that we live longer. It's about keeping our rivers and seas clean so that we can swim safely and drink the water without getting sick. It's about letting fruit and vegetables grow naturally so that we're not ingesting harmful chemicals. It's about protecting our ozone layer so that the sun – the very thing that gives life on our planet – doesn't end up being the cause of our demise. It's about reusing and recycling so that we're not amassing tonnes of ugly land fill or harming wildlife." I looked pleadingly at my dad. "All everyone is trying to do is create a better life for the human race. Why can't everyone stop fighting and start working together to accomplish that?"

He mulled over my words and then looked at me. "Did you have something in mind?"

I thought for a minute. "My great grandfather suggested something about increasing the population gradually. We could begin selective migration earlier than planned, which would give us more workers to help finish colonising the planet. As long as the number of immigrants was carefully managed so that resources weren't stretched... It should result in organic, incremental growth."

"When did you get so smart?"

"You can blame my new school."

"I'll have words with Mr Kepler when I see him next." He winked. "Nice idea in theory. How would we make it a reality?"

"Well, the people of Usonia would need to vote and agree on an early, gradual migration..."

"How would we get it to public vote?"

"All Usonians have the right to put proposals forward for referendum. I can do that. But do you think the other officials from Earth will agree to this compromise? Will it stall the government intervention? At least until it goes to public vote?"

"Leave that to me." He looked at his watch. "We'd better get back; the meeting will be resuming in ten minutes."

Dad stormed down the hill and I hurried after him.

"Where are you staying by the way?" I asked, short of breath.

"They've put us up at the hotel next to the transport interchange."

"Would you rather stay with me?"

He turned back. "I'd love to… If you're sure you don't mind?"

"Now that GG's gone, the house is kind of lonely. It would be nice to have you there."

"Well that's settled then. I'll collect my things from the hotel and come straight to you once this meeting's over."

When we got back to The Administration building, the government officials were solemnly filing into the meeting room. My dad gave me a meaningful look and then saluted me goodbye. I crossed my fingers on both hands and raised them for luck and then began circling the room to look for the rest of my class. I found them milling around near the door and Mr Kepler spotted me and waved me over.

"Ah, here she is! Everyone present and accounted for… We'd better get back to school before the rain comes."

The rest of the afternoon passed by in a blur. I couldn't concentrate on anything and Mr Kepler seemed to allow me to drift into my own world. I was sick with worry about what the government officials would say to my idea. I looked at my watch almost every minute, trying to push time forward with mental force. When the bell rang to signal the end of the day, I bounded out of my seat and headed straight for the door without a backward glance. I reached home in record time and burst through the door only to be greeted by an empty house. I paced around the living room, biting my nails, for as long as I could stand before turning on my heels and marching straight towards the garage door. I programmed the co-ordinates to the interchange hotel, jumped into the cap and sped off to find my father.

Minutes later, I hopped out at the hotel and strode towards the reception desk. "Could you please call Daniel Moore for me?" I started to ask before I'd even reached the receptionist.

"I'm afraid he hasn't returned from his meeting yet. Would you like me to take a message or would you prefer to wait in the lounge?" the male receptionist asked pleasantly.

I was already half way back to the cap by the time he'd finished his sentence, calling, "No, no thank you!" behind me.

I punched in the code for The Administration and within minutes I was climbing back out of the cap and running towards the meeting rooms. I almost skidded to a halt outside the door just as it swung open and a crowd of government officials spilled out of the room. Everyone looked disconcertingly pleased with themselves, and my stomach twisted. We'd lost. All of us. Usonians, the human race… We'd all lost.

Chapter 17

My shoulders slumped in desolation. I watched my dad walk out of the meeting room and as he saw me, his face broke into a smile. That manipulating liar. Everyone was right about him all along. I was a complete fool.

He headed straight towards me and raised his thumbs in the air. "We did it!"

I looked up. "What?"

"We did it!" He laughed. "Everyone agreed to your proposal. It was unanimous."

I ran over and threw my arms around him, squealing with laughter. Dad spun me around until we were both dizzy and collapsed on our backs on the nearby sofa.

"Let's not get ahead of ourselves," he said. "We still need to get the majority of Usonians to agree. Otherwise we're back to square one."

I frowned and looked at my watch. "We'd better get going; I've got work to do."

I worked on my proposal for half of the night, and then slept fitfully, my sleep interrupted by dreams that I was submerged in murky polluted waters or falling down never-ending canyons built from landfill waste on either side. I kept waking up either gasping for air or gripping onto the side of the bed in terror.

I awoke before sunrise and crept out of the house quietly so as not to wake my dad. I arrived at school just as it was opening and headed straight to my desk. I slid my jacket off as I sat down and began logging into The Administration's portal. I entered all of my details and then marked the proposal as high priority. I'd just about finished typing in my proposal when Mr Kepler walked through the door.

"You're early, Mia! You look terrible; is everything alright?"

I looked up from my frantic tapping and nodded, without stopping for a second. Once I'd entered the last few words, I called Mr Kepler over to check it for me.

"I'm very impressed, Mia. There's no doubt you're a McAdams."

"Will you endorse it for me? It says all high priority proposals need to be endorsed by another Usonian before The Administration will look at it ahead of other submissions."

"Of course. Just hit submit and I'll log in and do that straight away."

I sat back in relief and then a wave of tiredness seemed to hit me.

"Go home and rest, Mia, you look like you haven't slept a wink."

I opened my mouth to argue but a yawn slipped out instead. I reluctantly picked up my things and sloped back home to bed.

The next few days were agony. My father went back on the next flight later that day so I was left to my own devices all weekend. News had quickly broken about my talk with Conan. I'd never felt so popular, but I was too anxious for visitors. Both Stella and Noah tried to distract me but I must have been such terrible company that they both gave up in the end. By the time Monday came around, I was looking forward to school, purely as a way to take my mind off the proposal.

I was met by an excited buzz of chatter when I reached the classroom. I was the last to reach my seat and had just slipped off my jacket when Mr Kepler walked in, closing the door behind him.

"Good morning, class! I can tell by the racket coming down the hall that some of you have already heard the news this morning…."

I sat confused. What news? I started to regret not looking at the paper that morning. I was so preoccupied that the words kept swimming in front of my eyes and I'd had to put it down.

"I can tell from your expression, Miss McAdams, that you have no idea what I'm referring to," Mr Kepler said in his usual cheerful tone.

I shook my head.

"All Usonians have been issued with an impromptu referendum this morning. A high priority proposal has been submitted to The Administration and it will be put to vote this morning." He looked at me poignantly. "As usual, of course, we won't know the subject until the referendum commences in a few minutes' time."

My body tensed. This was it. It was make or break for the future of Usonia. I worried that people wouldn't understand the severity of their decision. That if the majority voted against early migration, Earth would intervene and life on Usonia as we know it would be over.

All screens flashed to life, beaming the adjudicator's image around the room. I had difficulty concentrating, I was so anxious.

"Good morning, fellow Usonians." Her clipped, robotic voice had everyone sitting upright in their seats instantly. "My name is Astrid Wright and I have the pleasure of acting as your adjudicator for today's referendum. Thank you for joining us today at such short notice. It is most unusual for referendums to be announced over the weekend - as you know - we Usonians value our leisure time infinitely. However, on this occasion, time is not on our side. You will have been aware that the government officials of Earth have been in meetings at The Administration for the past week. This referendum is the result of those meetings, and as part of the agreement, we have committed to vote on the subject today. Without further ado, today you will be asked to vote on the following topic." She cleared her throat. "The Administration proposes to commence migration from Earth, immediately." The entire room gasped in shock and my stomach sank. The adjudicator continued. "The proposal suggests we begin migration slowly and gradually, as a means to organically increase the rate of construction and production, without over-stretching resources and causing damage to our planet."

I breathed a silent sigh of relief and let my body relax. After she'd gone over the pros and the cons, our screens flashed up with the voting panel. The pros were on the left and listed: additional workers, population diversity, increased funding, and improved interplanetary relations. The cons were listed to the right: small population increase, small resource strain, increased construction, integration concerns.

When I looked at the proposal like that, stripped back and in black and white, it didn't look so clear cut. I suddenly wanted to leap up and scream out what the alternative was. It took all my strength of will to stay in my seat with my mouth tightly closed.

The adjudicator reminded us of the voting rules and then started the clock. I didn't waste a second, pressing 'Yes' firmly, the second that voting commenced. I sat upright in my seat and looked around to see my classmates' brows furrowed in concentration.

Stella was chewing her fingers, reading and rereading her screen. Al was hunched over his desk, agonising over his vote. I glanced at Noah but he was the only one sat back in his seat. Arms folded and expressionless. I watched as slowly, one by one, the remainder made their decisions. It was the longest five minutes of my life.

The countdown from ten began and our screens went blank as soon as voting closed. Everyone waited in pained silence while the votes were counted. I looked down at my hands in my lap and noticed that my knuckles had gone white, I was clenching them together so tightly. I didn't want to think about the consequences if the proposal wasn't passed. I closed my eyes and took slow deep breaths.

The classroom erupted with noise and my eye lids flicked open. It took a second for my eyes to adjust and focus, scanning the bar chart in front of me. One bar towered over the the others and my heart rate increased rapidly. I could hear it throbbing in my ears.

"Thank you for your patience, neighbours," the adjudicator spoke. "The results are in and I can confirm that the majority has voted in clear favour of the proposal. The migration from Earth will commence imminently. Thank you for voting and please have a wonderful day."

I let out an enormous breath that I hadn't realised I'd been holding and smiled with relief. Stella skipped over to my desk, pulled me up with both hands and then danced me around in circles.

Mr Kepler came over and shook my hand. "Well done, Mia, you should be very proud." He turned to the rest of the class. "Take five, class! We all deserve a few minutes to celebrate."

Everyone bustled excitedly out of the classroom but just as I reached the doorway, I felt a tug on my arm and I was pulled back into the room. Noah stood in front of me with an expression on his face that I hadn't seen before.

"You're amazing, do you know that?" His eyes were shining with admiration.

I shook my head, embarrassed.

"Well you are. What you did saved Usonia, and everything we stand for. We owe you *everything*."

I couldn't look him in the eye, I was so caught off guard by his close presence, by his words. And then I felt his fingers on my chin, tilting my face upwards so that I couldn't avoid meeting his gaze. His eyes softened and closed, and then suddenly his lips were on mine. A soft, warm, lingering kiss. A kiss that emptied my brain of all the thoughts that were swimming around my head. His hand pressed into my lower back, pulling me closer towards him and my body melted into his.

We were brought back to reality with a noisy cough. "I wondered where you two had disappeared to," Stella said rolling her eyes.

We broke apart and laughed, embarrassed. The room quickly filled with our noisy classmates and the spell was broken.

"Ok, class, who feels like learning some languages?" Mr Kepler asked, clapping his hands.

Over the next few weeks, everything seemed to settle into some form of normalcy. I was spending more and more time with Noah and Stella, and Priscilla had become almost like a surrogate mother to me.

My days had quickly become peacefully routine. I'd be awoken by the natural light and birdsong, and slowly wander into the kitchen. I'd select my breakfast and then while it was cooking, I'd read the paper with a glass of fresh juice. On weekdays, I'd walk into school with Stella and Noah, and on weekends, Priscilla would pick me up and take me to the markets. I hardly ever seemed to be alone in the evenings. I was making new friends every day, and I was always being invited somewhere for dinner. I finally felt like I truly belonged on Usonia.

Everyone was excited about the new arrivals from Earth and workers had gone into overdrive trying to make sure everything was ready for them. It seems silly now that I ever doubted the Usonians. They're such inherently good people that I should have known they would always have voted to help the people of Earth.

About six weeks after my dad left, I was scanning the paper before school, cramming scrambled eggs into my mouth as I read. I turned the page and my fork froze half way to my mouth, spilling the contents across the table. The headline announced that 20 presidents and prime ministers from Earth were to descend on Usonia today. I felt my entire body tense up. I couldn't believe it. After everything we'd done, they were still going to intervene? My fork dropped to the table and bounced to the floor. I pulled the paper closer and started to read the article without daring to breathe.

Stella barged excitedly through my door and I looked up. "Have you seen the news?" she asked, gasping for air.

"I'm just reading it now..." I looked at her questioningly.

"They're calling for volunteers to go to Earth. The governments need help preparing the people of Earth for future interplanetary integration. Anyone willing to help out needs to report to The Administration now." She paused for breath. "Are you in?"

She waited for my response, her face beaming with excitement. Stella wouldn't survive a day alone on Earth. There was no way I could let her go without me.

I steeled myself. "Ok... You can count me in."

Acknowledgements

Without the following people, this book would never have become a reality, and for that, I am grateful beyond words.

Firstly, I'd like to thank my dad, Kevin Gibbons, for instilling in me a love of literature and language from as early an age as I can remember. His encouragement, enthusiasm, support and faith in this project has meant so much to me.

I can't thank my mum, Janette Gibbons, enough for actually making this book happen. She encouraged me to start afresh and move back to Wales, housing and feeding me, so that I could dedicate my time to writing.

I need to thank my brother, Tony Gibbons, for simultaneously being my harshest critic and biggest fan. Without his relentless enthusiasm, brilliant ideas and brutal feedback, Project Ark wouldn't be a patch on the book it is today.

A big thank you to my sister, Corinne Gibbons, who read the book in its first draft, cried in all the right bits and didn't hold back in telling me which parts made her eyes glaze over. She is a big believer in following your passion and dreams and has been an enormous creative inspiration.

To Ben and Maddy at Nodding Dog, for bearing with my craziness while they designed a book cover that needed to match a year's worth of my figurative blood, sweat and tears. What they've created is awe-inspiring and far beyond my high expectations.

To my fellow writers, Pam Griffin, Danielle Williams-Smith and Will Jelbert, for being a wonderful source of advice, inspiration and encouragement.

To those of my friends who have had to put up with my contrasting bouts of hermitude and hedonistic procrastination over the past year, but stuck by me throughout it all.

And lastly, I'd like to thank James Zabiela. Not just because I owe him an acknowledgement, but because he's easily the coolest sci-fi nerd around.

Thank you x

Made in the USA
Charleston, SC
09 January 2015